The Prince

Also from Jennifer L. Armentrout

Forever With You
Dream of You (a 1001 Dark Nights Novel)
Fall With Me
Fire In You

By J. Lynn
Stay With Me
Be With Me
Wait For You

The Covenant Series
Daimon
Half-Blood
Pure
Deity
Elixer
Apollyon

The Lux Series
Shadows
Obsidian
Onyx
Opal
Origin
Opposition

The Origin Series
The Darkest Star

The Dark Elements
Bitter Sweet Love
White Hot Kiss
Stone Cold Touch
Every Last Breath

The Prince
A Wicked Novella

By Jennifer L. Armentrout

1001 Dark Nights

EVIL EYE
CONCEPTS

The Prince
A Wicked Novella
By Jennifer Armentrout

1001 Dark Nights
Copyright 2018 Jennifer Armentrout
ISBN: 978-1-948050-13-5

Foreword: Copyright 2014 M. J. Rose
Published by Evil Eye Concepts, Incorporated

Acknowledgments from the Author

Thank you to the team at 1001 Dark Nights, especially Liz Berry for inviting me to be a part of this amazing family of authors and Jillian Stein, for the beautiful friendship that has come with it and for making sure that I'll always be able to see the stars.

Sign up for the 1001 Dark Nights Newsletter
and be entered to win a Tiffany Key necklace.

There's a contest every month!

Go to www.1001DarkNights.com to subscribe.

As a bonus, all subscribers will receive a free copy of
Discovery Bundle Three
Featuring stories by
Sidney Bristol, Darcy Burke, T. Gephart
Stacey Kennedy, Adriana Locke
JB Salsbury, and Erika Wilde

One Thousand and One Dark Nights

Once upon a time, in the future...

I was a student fascinated with stories and learning.
I studied philosophy, poetry, history, the occult, and
the art and science of love and magic. I had a vast
library at my father's home and collected thousands
of volumes of fantastic tales.

I learned all about ancient races and bygone
times. About myths and legends and dreams of all
people through the millennium. And the more I read
the stronger my imagination grew until I discovered
that I was able to travel into the stories... to actually
become part of them.

I wish I could say that I listened to my teacher
and respected my gift, as I ought to have. If I had, I
would not be telling you this tale now.
But I was foolhardy and confused, showing off
with bravery.

One afternoon, curious about the myth of the
Arabian Nights, I traveled back to ancient Persia to
see for myself if it was true that every day Shahryar
(Persian: شهريار, "king") married a new virgin, and then
sent yesterday's wife to be beheaded. It was written
and I had read, that by the time he met Scheherazade,
the vizier's daughter, he'd killed one thousand
women.

Something went wrong with my efforts. I arrived in the midst of the story and somehow exchanged places with Scheherazade — a phenomena that had never occurred before and that still to this day, I cannot explain.

Now I am trapped in that ancient past. I have taken on Scheherazade's life and the only way I can protect myself and stay alive is to do what she did to protect herself and stay alive.

Every night the King calls for me and listens as I spin tales. And when the evening ends and dawn breaks, I stop at a point that leaves him breathless and yearning for more. And so the King spares my life for one more day, so that he might hear the rest of my dark tale.

As soon as I finish a story... I begin a new one... like the one that you, dear reader, have before you now.

Chapter 1

Did it make you a bad friend if you were completely, a hundred percent envious of that friend? Yes? No? Kind of?

I figured it was somewhere in between.

That's what I was mulling over as I watched Ivy Morgan brush thick, red curls over her shoulder, laughing at something her boyfriend Ren Owens had said to her.

At least I wasn't envious of that—their love. Okay, well, that wasn't entirely true. Pretty sure anyone who was as single as me would be envious of all that warm and fuzzy that was passed back and forth with each long look or casual brush of skin. The two could barely tear their gazes away from one another to eat the dinner we'd grabbed at the cute little diner inside the shopping center on Prytania Street.

I honest to God couldn't be happier for them. They'd been through so much—way more than two people should ever have to go through to be together, and here they were, stronger and more in love than ever, and they deserved that happiness.

But their epic love story wasn't the source of a current case of the green-eye monster that was sitting on my shoulder.

Ivy was just such a… badass.

Even right now, relaxed in the chair, surrounded by twinkling Christmas lights with her hand in Ren's and her belly full of a cheeseburger deluxe and crinkle fries and half of my tater tots, she could kick ass and take names along with addresses, telephone numbers, and social security numbers.

If the proverbial poo hit the fan, you called Ivy or Ren.

If you needed to know what streets Royal intersected with, you called… me. Or if you needed coffee or fresh beignets but were currently busy, you know, saving the world, you'd call me.

The three of us were all members of the Order, a widespread organization that was literally the only thing that stood between mankind and complete, utter enslavement and destruction by the fae. And not the super cute fae found in Disney movies or some crap like that. Humans thought they were on top of the food chain. They were wrong. The fae were.

The only thing pop culture got right about the fae was their slightly pointy ears. That was it. The fae were more than just beings from another world—the Otherworld—they were capable of glamouring their appearance to blend in with humans. But all Order members, even me, were warded at birth against the glamour. We saw through the human façade to the creature that lurked beneath.

No amount of imagination could capture their allure in their true form or how luminous their silvery skin was or how they were beautiful in the way a leopard stalking its prey was.

The fae preyed on humans—on the very life force that kept our hearts beating and brains working. Much like the mythical vampire feeding on blood or a succubus feasting on energy, the life force that they stole from humans fueled their abilities, which truly ran the gamut. They were faster and stronger than us, and nothing on Earth rivaled their predatory skills. Feeding off humans was also the way the fae slowed their aging process down to a lifespan that rivaled immortality. Without feeding, they aged and died like humans.

There were some of them who didn't feed on humans, something we'd only discovered recently. The fae from the Summer Court chose not to. They lived and died like us, wanting nothing more than to be left alone and out of the crosshairs of their enemies, the Winter fae.

My fingers drifted to my wrist, where I wore a bracelet that, combined with the words spoken at our births, held the charm that blocked the fae's ability. I never took the thing off. Ever.

Four leaf clovers.

Who ever would've thought a tiny plant would negate something as powerful as a fae?

But a week ago tonight the Order, along with the Summer fae, had done the impossible. The psychotic and wholly creepy fae Queen who went by the name Morgana had been sent back to the Otherworld. She could come back, but no one was expecting her to. Not for a long time. Maybe not even in our lifetime, but the Order would be ready when she did. So would the Summer fae.

That's why the three of us were having dinner—a little celebratory dinner. We'd survived the battle with the Queen and those who supported her had crawled back into whatever cesspools they were hiding in. We all could take a deep breath now and chill out, knowing that while there was still a metric crap ton of Winter fae out there who needed to be hunted down and stopped, we'd leveled out the playing field with the Queen's defeat.

Things were as normal as they'd ever be for an Order member. Hell, Ren and Ivy were even planning to take a vacation after Christmas. How crazy was that? Super crazy!

I wasn't planning a vacation, because I hadn't really taken part in the battle. If I had, I wouldn't be sitting here. I'd be dead. Like clinically, irreversibly dead.

I'd only received minimal combat training before that had come to a grinding halt when I was twelve. And while I still took the Order-mandated training classes along with Ivy, I've never seen any real action. Working through take-down maneuvers or knowing how to avoid a punch or a deliver a bone-snapping kick was completely different than actually taking that knowledge and using it against someone who was actively trying to straight-up murder you.

If my life hadn't veered off track at twelve, I would've been just like Ivy and Ren—a walking weapon on two legs–but everything had changed when my mother had been captured by the fae she'd been hunting.

My mother was a fighter, much like my father, who'd died when I was too young to remember him beyond the photographs that hung in the hallway. She had been one of the greatest, most skilled fighters in the Order - dare I say, even more badass than Ivy. She'd raised me while still pulling all nighters, patrolling the streets of New Orleans for fae, hunting them before they could hunt humans. When I was younger, I swore I was going to be just like her—like every child raised in the Order planned. We were indoctrinated at birth and our duty to protect mankind was what all of us prepared for. Training started young, at the age of eight. Mornings were dedicated to schooling and afternoons were part learning about the habits of the fae and part training.

But then came the morning, when I was a few days shy of my twelfth birthday, that Mom… she hadn't come home. Those days that had followed, those days that felt like an eternity, were some of the worst memories I will ever have.

Mom had been found on day four, in one of the bayous several miles out from the city, left for dead. Even as skilled as she was, she had fallen to the fae. They'd tortured her. Worse yet, they had fed on her, and while they hadn't enslaved her, all those feedings had done something to her. To her mind. Thank God, my mom had come home to me.

But she hadn't come home the same.

There'd been days and weeks where it was like nothing had happened to her, and then things weren't okay. She'd just up and disappear one day or would refuse to come out of her room. She'd rant and rage and then break into fits of laughter that would last hours. Things got easier in the months and years following her attack, but taking care of her had replaced training, and when I came of age, I was given an administrator-type job with the Order, something reserved for the lucky few that made it to retirement. I accepted it even though the money the Order had paid out to my mother for her 'injured in the line of duty' situation was substantial.

But I was hoping that could change now. Things were going to simmer down, and I was hoping with a little more training, I could start patrolling. The Order needed me—needed all the help they could get since so many had been lost in the battle with the Queen. I could become just as badass as Ivy and Ren and then I'd finally be able to fulfill my duty.

I'd finally be… useful. Worthy of those I called my friends and, most importantly, worthy of the legacy of my family. I could—

Fingers appeared directly in my line of vision. They snapped, causing me to jerk back in my seat. The fingers lowered to reveal Ivy staring at me.

My cheeks heated as I laughed softly. "Sorry. I spaced out. Were you saying something?"

"I was saying that I was about to strip naked and run outside."

Ren's green eyes practically twinkled. "I am so down for that."

"Of course you are." Grinning, she gestured at the menu. "Did you want dessert, Bri?"

Only Ivy called me Bri. Everyone else called me Brighton or Ms. Jussier. I hated the latter. It made me feel like I was three decades older and should be living in a home full of stray, un-neutered cats. And I was already twenty-eight and living with my mother. I didn't need to feel worse than I already did.

"No, I'm good." I'd already peeked at the menu. If they had cheesecake, I would've made room.

Ren glanced over the menu and then shook his head as he handed it back to Ivy. "So, you going to let Tink move in with you?"

I nearly choked on the sip of diet Coke. "What?"

Dropping the menu on the table, Ivy smiled as she clasped her hands together. "If Ren and I go on vacation, Tink's going to need an adult in his life."

I opened my mouth, but I had no words. I could not have heard them right. No way could I move Tink into my house—my mother's house—because not only would Tink most likely destroy it, he was....

Well, Tink was Tink.

"And he really likes you," Ren added. "He actually listens to you."

My brows lowered. "That's not true. Tink listens to no one. Not even his boyfriend. And why wouldn't he stay with him?"

"Well, I made that suggestion, and according to Tink, he's not ready for that kind of commitment," Ren replied dryly.

"What? That's not a commitment," I reasoned. "It would only be temporary, right?"

"We tried explaining that to Tink." Ivy rolled her eyes. "But you know how he is."

I didn't. I really didn't. I lowered my voice so we weren't overheard. "Why can't he stay at Hotel Good Fae?" That was what Ivy called the compound the Summer fae lived in. "They *love* him. Like near worship levels."

"We suggested that, but he said, and I quote, he can't 'be himself' around them. That their admiration is too much pressure on him."

I stared at Ren. "You're joking."

"I wish." He leaned back. "You know we can't leave him alone. He'd burn down Ivy's apartment."

"He'll spend all my money on shit from Amazon," Ivy added as her phone rang. She picked up her bag. "Anyway, we'll talk out the details later."

We were so not talking out the details later. "But—"

"What's up, Miles?" Ivy held her hand up, and I snapped my mouth shut. "What?" She glanced at Ren, who was alert and all eyes on Ivy. "Yeah, we're nearby. We can check it out." There was a pause. "I'll update you in a few."

Disconnecting the call, she pulled out her wallet and said, "Miles said Gerry didn't show up for his shift and no one can get ahold of him," she explained, and that wasn't normal at all. Gerry was habitually on time. "He asked if we could swing by his place and check things out."

"Can do," Ren answered as Ivy dropped several bills on the table. "By the way, I'm pretty sure Tink is at your place now with Merle."

"Wait. What?" I immediately forgot about Gerry not showing up for patrol.

"Yeah, he said something about wanting gardening tips or something bizarre." Ivy shoved her wallet into her bag. "Honestly, I wasn't really listening."

"Oh God." I fumbled for my wallet as visions of my mom impaling Tink with steak knives danced in my head. "He cannot be there alone with my mom."

"I think Merle likes Tink," Ivy said.

"Really?" I dropped cash on the table—more than enough cover my food and a tip. "Depends on if he's Tink-size or people-size."

"I feel the same way," Ren muttered, and then he slid a sly glance in my direction. "By the way, I'm pretty sure your mom has the hots for Tanner."

I was frozen, halfway standing. Tanner ran Hotel Good Fae. In other words, he was a fae and my mom—well, Mom did seem to like visiting him, but she also talked quite frequently about killing fae, all kinds of fae. Shaking my head, I decided I really didn't have the brain space to process any of that. "I better get going. God only knows what my mom and Tink could get into."

"I figure it'll either be epic or epically disastrous." Ivy grinned at me as she and Ren stood.

"Agreed." Wishing they had mentioned all of this at the beginning of dinner, I slung my purse over my shoulder and said my goodbyes.

Hurrying through the small diner and skirting the oversized Christmas tree, I made my way outside. Cool wind caught the fine strands of hair around my face, blowing my ponytail over my shoulder. I lived a handful of blocks from the shopping center, and it was quicker just to walk instead of trying to order an Uber.

Shoving my hands into the front pocket of my oversized hoodie, I jogged across the street. The Garden District was beautiful any time of year, but it really amped up its curb appeal during the Christmas season. Lights of all different colors decorated porches and balconies, twisted around wrought iron fences, and twinkled from the massive oaks that lined many of the streets.

I could not believe Tink was at my place. What in the world were Ivy and Ren thinking? Mom didn't hate Tink, but Mom had also, at one time, suggested to Ivy's face that Ivy should be put down.

All because Ivy wasn't exactly a hundred percent human. She was a halfling and there had been this whole prophecy that involved her permanently opening the gates to the Otherworld, allowing the armies of the Winter Court to enter our world, but all of that was over. Thank God.

And Tink was definitely not even one percent human.

Cutting down a side street, I tried not to let my imagination run wild with what could be happening at home. They could be sitting together and watching Harry Potter. Or Tink could've brought his boyfriend, who just happened to be Prince Fabian—one of the two Princes of the Summer Court—to the house. I doubted Tink would've brought Prince Fabian's brother with him. At least there was that.

A shudder racked my shoulders as an image of *the* Prince formed in my head. I'd never seen him when he was under the Queen's enchantment, masquerading as the Winter Prince. He'd terrorized the city, becoming a living and breathing nightmare who had kidnapped Ivy to fulfill said prophecy.

I'd only seen him after the enchantment was broken, and even then he'd been the most intimidating creature I'd ever laid eyes on. And when he looked at me, I couldn't help but feel—

"Mom." My steps drew up short as I spotted her coming down the wide sidewalk, her thin housecoat flapping behind her like wings. "What are you doing out here?"

She stepped under the street lamp, her short blond hair messy from the wind. "Oh, I was just getting… antsy and decided I wanted to go for a walk."

I hurried to where she stood, taking her hands in mine. Her skin was cold. "Mom, why didn't you put on your jacket?"

"Honey, it's not that cold outside." She laughed, squeezing my hands.

"It's cold enough for something heavier than this robe you've got going on. Let's head back home." My stomach twisted with nerves as I looped my arm through hers and turned her back around.

Anxiety and the inability to stay still was usually a sign that we were about to hit a rough couple of days. It came out of nowhere and nothing and everything could trigger it. She would go from being clear minded and sharp as a tack for weeks, months even, and then wham! She would start roaming off and then the nightmares would start. She wouldn't be able to sleep and things would…they would just spiral.

Worry was like a virus. By the time you felt it, you were already drowning in it. "How long have you been outside?"

"Long enough to walk from the house to here," she replied, and I resisted the urge to roll my eyes. "And what's wrong with my robe?"

There were several things wrong with her roaming around the Garden District in a robin's egg blue robe.

I slowed my pace to match hers as I guided her across the street. "Did you have company while I was gone?"

"Company?"

Maybe Ren and Ivy were wrong about Tink being there. "Did Tink come by?" I asked, starting to get nervous.

She was quiet for a moment and then she chuckled. "Actually, come to think of it, he was watching a movie and then he stepped outside to make a phone call."

"So, he was still there when you—" The street lamp above us flickered once and then faded out.

All the way down the block, as far as I could see, the lights flickered and then disappeared.

"That's odd," Mom commented, a shiver working its way through her. "Brighton?"

"It's okay," I said, swallowing hard. "Everything is okay."

A blast of what felt like arctic air swept down the block, lifting the edges of Mom's housecoat and stopping both of us in our tracks. The tiny hairs all along the nape of my neck rose as I scanned the empty street, only lit by the faint, twinkling Christmas lights. I recognized the for sale sign in front of the empty antebellum home. We had another two blocks to go.

"Mom," I whispered, heart pounding in my chest as I started walking again, dragging her along with me. "We need to—"

They seemed to come out of nowhere, moving so fast they were nothing more than shadows at first, surrounding us.

A scream built in my throat as I saw them. Silvery skin. Eyes filled with hate. Four of them, and they were on us before the scream could even part my lips.

Chapter 2

Sunlight.

That's what I felt on my skin and tasted on my lips. *Sunlight*. Its warmth seeped through my skin, buzzed through my veins, and settled into my muscles and bones.

Was I lying outside? That wouldn't make sense, though. It was December, and not nearly warm enough to sunbathe, but I knew I had to be lying close to the sun. I could feel its touch on my cheek and my lips still tingled from the closeness.

I opened my eyes, but I didn't see the sun. I saw a form... a shape of a man. The features blurred, but I knew the man. It was him.

The Prince....

But that also didn't make sense. None of this made sense. Confusion crept into the fuzz crowding my thoughts. Something was off. I tried to lift my hand, but my arm felt like it was weighted down. Something was wrong, very badly wrong, and I needed to remember—

Sleep.

The desire to slip away hit me hard and fast, obliterating the confusion and consciousness, and I slept. I slept for what felt like years and then I heard a steady beeping. It intruded on wherever I was, becoming so loud, so obnoxious to me, that I had to pay attention to it. A part of my consciousness zeroed in on the sound, clung to it, and I followed it back, tethering myself to the rhythm. With each passing second, my surroundings became clearer. Footsteps. I heard footsteps. Whispers. There was the sound of hushed voices. I dragged in a deep breath, and a shock hit my system. The breath *hurt*. Like my chest and ribs were too tight and a simple deep breath was too much to take—

Mom.

I saw her in my mind, as clear as day.

I saw her lying on her back in the darkness, her eyes wide and fixed on mine. There was nothing behind those eyes. No life. Nothing.

The beeping sound sped up.

The horrifying image of my mom faded like smoke, replaced by luminous skin and bloody smiles and taunts and...

Pools of blood. Actual pools of it. The ruby-red liquid spilled across stone, forming rivulets that ran between the spacing in the pavers. Why had there been so much blood? A vague feeling of wet warmth bubbling up my throat and choking me swept through me.

"Bri? Are you awake? Brighton?"

I recognized that voice. Ivy. She was speaking to me, and I took another breath, relieved to discover it didn't hurt as bad as the first. But my... my body felt weird. My face felt weird. Like it was swollen and stretched too tight. It was the same with every inch of my skin.

My eyes felt like they were glued shut, and it took forever for them to open. Hours maybe. But when they did, I found myself staring at a drop ceiling and florescent lights.

"Bri." Ivy spoke again, and her fingers lightly brushed my left hand.

Slowly, I turned my head toward the sound of her voice, to my left, and I saw her pale, drawn face. All that bright hair was pulled back in a bun. Her eyes were red and swollen and full of sympathy.

And I knew.

I *remembered*.

The fae had come out of nowhere, surrounding Mom and me. They'd dragged us into the courtyard of the empty house. There hadn't been four of them. I'd been wrong. There'd been five and one of them had been an Ancient.

I swallowed, or tried to, but the motion hurt my throat. *Everything* hurt. My legs and face, but especially my stomach. That felt like someone had dug around inside and pulled everything out.

Ivy's fingers curled around mine. She squeezed gently. "Are you in pain? I can get the doc."

I squeezed my eyes shut, and I saw flashes of teeth and razor-sharp claws. The fae didn't need to use their teeth to feed, but they liked to use them to cause pain.

"Mom," I croaked out, and Ivy's hand spasmed around mine. When she didn't answer, I forced my eyes open again. "She's... she's gone?"

Ivy pressed her lips together as she nodded jerkily. "I'm sorry. I'm so sorry, Bri."

My gaze dropped to where Ivy held my hand. Instead of seeing her hand, I saw my mother's blood-soaked one squeezing mine. I saw it slip from my grasp as I felt the strength seep out of her.

"They made several hits, all across the city," Ivy was saying, curling her other hand around mine, clasping it between her two palms. "That's why Gerry didn't show up for his shift. Ren and I found him. That's when we knew." Her voice turned hoarse as she started naming names—names of those killed and there were so many, an endless stream. "They must've been watching us. They knew where to go. So much violence, all in one night."

Ivy dropped her forehead to her hands. I didn't see her, though. I saw the five faces. I remembered their faces. I would always remember their faces.

"You're going to be okay. The doc says it's a freaking miracle, but you're going to be okay," she said. "They'll probably keep you for a couple more days, but then you can come home with me, if you want. Tink said you can take his bedroom—"

"I... I couldn't stop them."

"What?" Ivy lifted her head. Her eyes were glassy.

"I... I couldn't fight them off."

She slowly shook her head. "Bri, you were hunted down and—"

"I couldn't stop them!" The shout tore at my raw throat, but I didn't care. "They killed my mother and I couldn't stop them!"

"No." Ivy rose, leaning over the head of the bed so her face was right in mine. "I know what you're thinking. Trust me, I *know*. This is not your fault. I would've been screwed if I was caught off guard and surrounded like that."

I didn't think that was the case. Ivy would've fought tooth and nail. She wouldn't have panicked and flailed. She wouldn't have let them get her on her back, the number one thing they taught you to never let happen in training. Ivy might've struggled, but she would've prevailed.

"What they did to your mom and you is on them." Ivy placed the tips of her fingers against my cheek. The touch was light, as if she knew if she pressed too hard, it would hurt. "There was nothing you could've done, Bri. Nothing. You survived. That's all that matters. And it's going to be okay. Everything is going to be okay."

As I stared at her, remembering what I'd said to Mom, and knowing that it had been a lie, I knew that this also wasn't true. That wasn't all that mattered and it wasn't going to be okay.

Things were never going to be okay.

Chapter 3

Two years later....

The heavy, rhythmic beat thumped from the speakers above and flowed over the packed floor. Gleaming bodies twisted and churned under the flashing overhead lights, lost to the music and the press of flesh against flesh. The scent of perfume, cologne, and sweat turned my stomach as I lifted my hands, scooping the long strands of hair off my damp neck.

Tonight I was a wild redhead with bright, red lips.

Last night I'd been a raven-haired seductress with smokey eyes.

The past weekend I was a naïve blonde in pigtails with flushed, peachy cheeks.

Each time I was someone different, but I was always the perfect victim, and every night ended the same.

I swayed my hips to the beat, to the hard, warm body behind me as I scanned the dance floor, searching.

Hands moved over the silvery sequins of my dress, slipping over my stomach. He hauled me against him, pressing his front to my back.

He was *really* into this.

A lot.

Those questing hands dragged down my hips, inching closer to my outer thighs. Letting go of the hair, I caught his wrists and tossed a reckless grin over my shoulder. "Behave."

The nameless man gave me a toothy smile. He was cute, definitely younger than me by a good decade and some change. Probably in college at Loyola or Tulane, which meant two things. He'd choke if he knew I was pushing thirty-one and this was the last place he should be. A tiny part of me wanted to warn him, to tell him to find his fun and pleasure anyplace but the club Flux.

But I wasn't here for him.

Holding onto his wrists, I let my head fall back against his chest as my gaze flickered over the dance floor and the horseshoe-shaped bar at the front. I couldn't see into the shadowy alcoves surrounding the floor or upstairs, on the second floor VIP area.

That's where I needed to be, because I knew *he* was up there.

A squat, broad man blocked the staircase. Behind him was a red rope. Entry to the second floor was by invite only, and those up there didn't come down here. They sent scouts instead, scouts that were trained to find a certain type of human.

And I was the living embodiment of that type and tonight was the night.

"Hey," the man said into my ear.

I kept searching. "Yeah?"

"What's your name? I'm Dale." He tried to move his hands again, but I kept them on my hips.

"Sally," I lied as a tall, slender woman at the bar pushed away and turned to the dance floor, a vibrant, too-bright purple drink in her hand. Nightshade. She lifted the drink to her lips as she stared out over the floor.

I'd found who I was searching for, and I saw her for what she really looked like.

"You wanna get out of here, Sally?" Dale asked, his lips brushing the side of my neck. "I know a place we can go to."

"No, thank you." Letting go of his wrists, I pulled away from the man, walking off and slipping between the bodies before his shocked expletive could get under my skin.

Keeping an eye on the scout, I eased around a couple who were practically mating right there on the floor. I couldn't tell where one of them ended and the other began.

Goodness.

I passed a high, round top table, plucked up the forgotten, half empty pink drink, and made a beeline for the bar. As soon as I stepped out of the cluster of bodies, I slowed my step and fixed a lax smile on my face as I neared the female. She wasn't focused on me, instead eyeing two young college girls who were dancing and laughing, obviously buzzing. She started toward them.

Letting the borrowed glass dangle from my fingers, I tripped, bumping my shoulder against the female.

She turned to me in a slow, calculated snake-like movement. Her lips peeled back in a sneer as she lowered her glass of nightshade. To everyone else in this club, her smile appeared normal. To me? I saw the two wickedly sharp incisors on each side of her mouth. Not fangs. Just sharp as an obsidian blade teeth that could tear through flesh.

"I'm so sorry." I teetered on my high heels as I spoke over the music, placing my free hand on her arm. "Someone bumped me. Ugh. People are so rude."

She lifted a single dark eyebrow.

"What in the world are you drinking? It looks *sooo* amazing."

The female cocked her head to the side as her pale blue eyes drifted over every inch of my body, from the thick red hair and bright lips to the plunging neckline of my strappy silvery dress that showed off more than it hid. She must've approved of what she saw, because a tight-lipped smile replaced her sneer. "This drink is a little too hard for you."

"Oh?" I bit down on my lower lip. "I like... hard drinks, though."

"Do you?" When I nodded, the female stepped closer. She was my height, so her gaze lined up with mine. "How hard do you like it?"

"Very hard," I repeated, forcing myself to hold her gaze as I giggled.

She tilted her head slightly. "I might have something better for you. You here alone?"

"My friends already left. I was getting ready to go, but... I think I have another good hour or so left in me."

"Perfect." The moment her black pupils constricted was brief and not noticeable to anyone who didn't know better, but I did. I knew what she was doing, entrancing me. I forced my muscles to loosen, for the eager smile that said I was down for anything to slip off my face. I stood before the female, silent... and waiting as she leaned in, brushing her lips against mine as she whispered, "Come with me."

She plucked the borrowed drink out of my hand and placed it on the bar beside us, then she took my hand in her cool grasp. Her pace was fast and steps long as she led me around the bar to the staircase.

Jackpot.

The man standing at the foot of the stairs stepped aside, and one glance at his vacant expression told me he was a human that had been fed on until he was completely under the fae's control. And just as dangerous and unpredictable as the fae themselves.

She led me up the wide spiral staircase, her grip tight as she all but dragged me along, turning right at the top to a dimly lit balcony. Downing half of the nightshade, a drink toxic to humans but more like tequila to the fae, she led me to a set of occupied couches and chair. I registered several fae, all with a tranced human by their side or in their laps. It was likely none of these humans were going to make it out of this club alive tonight.

"Look what I found, Tobias." The female pulled me forward with a strength that didn't match her willowy frame, and I let myself be shoved, even allowed myself to stumble. The fae caught my arm, stopping me from toppling flat on my face.

My gaze darted around, and then I saw *him*.

He was sitting on a small, black couch, his arms and legs spread in an arrogant sprawl. I saw the human façade just for a brief second. Pale skin gave way to a silvery tone. Hair and features remained the same. Blond and handsome, he looked like a frat boy with silver skin and pointed ears. He was definitely one of *them*.

And now I had a name to match a face I'd never forget.

Tobias.

A rush of anticipation shot through my veins, spreading goosebumps all over my skin. It was him. There'd been five of them total and he was one of the three that remained.

"You always treat me well, Alyssa," he said, his pale blue gaze crawling over my length. "You know how I have a soft spot for redheads."

"A soft spot." The female fae called Alyssa let go of my arm. "More like a hard-on."

Oh dear.

I kept my face impressively blank as Tobias jerked his chin. Oscar worthy, really. Another fae came forward, out of the shadows. He was a tall one and it took everything in me not to flinch as he put his hands on me, skimming them down my front and back, checking for weapons. The fae had gotten smarter in the last two years.

So had we.

The fae's hands moved up my legs meticulously and then my hips. His fingers glanced over the wide cuffs at my wrists. "She's clear."

"Good." Tobias leaned forward. "Come here, Red."

I forced my steps to be slow and uneven, and when he lifted his hand to me, I placed mine in his even though it utterly sickened me.

Tobias didn't pull me into his lap like I expected. Instead, he rose from the couch. "What time will Aric be here?"

Aric? That name wasn't familiar to me; then again, it wasn't like I hung out with these murderous, psychotic Winter fae.

"You have an hour, tops." Alyssa tossed herself onto the couch. "Make good use of it."

"You bet." He circled his arm around my waist, drawing me to his front. He smelled good. Like winter mint. But they all smelled good. They all looked good, too. And this fae was obviously in the mood for more than just feeding, which was what I was betting on. "You want seconds?"

"Sure," the female fae purred. "If there's anything left."

Tobias lifted me up without warning, tossing me over his shoulder like a damn Neanderthal claiming his prize. To go limp scratched at my skin as he stalked across the short distance. A door opened and then we were inside a room that I imagined a lot of very bad things happened in. He kicked the door shut behind us and I heard the lock turn without him touching it.

His hand curved over my ass as he lowered me onto the floor. Strands of red hair had fallen in front of my face, and I stood there as he brushed them back behind my ears. "Do you know why I like redheads? No. Of course you don't."

I blinked slowly, taking in the room as he let go. There was a chair. A bed that looked... well used. My stomach churned with nausea. But he didn't go to the bed; he went to the throne-like chair with crushed velvet cushions. He sat and stared up at me.

"Come on. Don't be shy." Those pale eyes seemed to burn. "We're going to get to know each other, aren't we?"

"Yes?" I whispered.

A half smile spread across his lips as he hooked a finger in my direction. "Come on then."

I forced a small smile as I shuffled to him. The gasp was real when he grabbed my hips and tugged me down into his lap, causing the skirt to ride up my thighs. He toyed with the straps of my dress, tracing the low v-shaped neckline.

"You want me?" he asked.

That was an odd, unnecessary question. Guess someone had a low sense of self worth or something. "Yes."

"You'll let me do anything to you, won't you?"

I forced myself to nod. "*Yes.*"

"Then touch me," he ordered softly.

My jaw clenched as I placed my hands on his shoulders, smoothing them over his chest.

"Honestly, I really don't like redheads." His hand moved fast, closing around my throat. "I hate them."

Oh, hell.

He squeezed not too gently, digging his fingers into my windpipe as he drew me forward. His icy breath danced over my lips as I winced at the spike of pain. "Why?" His other hand was on the move, sliding down my spine, going lower. "They remind me of the bitch halfling."

I knew exactly who he was talking about.

Ivy Morgan—wait, she was Ivy Owens now, having gotten married over Christmas to Ren.

Then, before I had a chance to process what he was doing, his cold mouth was on mine. Lips. Teeth. Tongue. It was harsh and brutal, and I wondered if he even knew how to kiss or if he cared. He let go of my throat, and I figured there'd be bruises there later.

I held still as he eased the straps of my dress down my arms, fueled by one of the most powerful emotions known to man.

Vengeance.

I was so close to retribution, I could taste the bitter sweetness of it on the tip of my tongue. It burned through the iciness his kiss left behind.

The top slipped, pooling low on my hips and exposing the black, seriously uncomfortable strapless bra. My gaze fixed on the ceiling as his cool lips skated down the column of my throat and then lower, over the swell of my breast. I forced my body to stay loose, accepting even as the tips of his fingers skated over my sides to where the material bunched. His fingers brushed the thin, silver chain that rode low around my hips.

Tobias drew back, and I could practically feel his gaze roam over my chest and then my stomach, and I knew what he saw. Not smooth, unmarred skin. Pale, shiny scars that covered the entirety of my stomach. Teeth marks. Multiple ones that had healed and faded to a shade or two lighter than my normal skin. Deep groves made by sharpened claws. All of them a permanent reminder of the night nearly two years ago when the fae who'd supported the defeated Winter Queen had sought bloody vengeance and commenced wholesale slaughter. They hadn't even fed on us. They'd just wanted us to hurt.

And we did.

The night my mother, who had already suffered so much at the hands of the fae, had died, nearly ripped apart by their teeth and claws.

The night I should've died.

His hands clenched my hips, digging into my skin. "What the hell?"

I lowered my chin as he tugged on the chain and the small, circle medallion pulled free from the dress. I knew the exact moment he recognized the encased four-leaf clover. Tobias knew what that meant.

I wasn't under his glamour.

Tobias's pale, furious gaze flew to mine. I smiled then. "Remember me?"

Powerful muscles coiled underneath me as recognition flared in those eyes, but I was faster than I had been that night, than I had been for my entire life, and the Order had gotten smarter at hiding our weapons. I twisted my right wrist and the wide cuff bracelet disengaged a collapsible iron stake. The deadly metal shot out over the palm of my hand. Clutching his shoulder, I jabbed my right arm out, slamming the iron stake deep into the fae's chest.

Surprise parted his lips as he gasped out, "Bitch."

"Yeah."

Then it happened.

As quick as a heartbeat, the sick bastard collapsed into himself as he was sucked back into the Otherworld, locked away and as good as dead to me. Falling forward, I caught myself on the back of the chair, my knees slipping across the cushion. I disengaged the stake, hearing the mechanical click as it folded back into the bracelet.

Dragging in a deep breath, I held it as I squeezed my eyes shut. There had been five of them that had found my mother and me. Five of them that had gone after an old woman and her daughter. Three were now as good as dead, and that left two more. A fae and a—

An odd thump hit the wall outside of the room, causing my eyes to snap open. Pushing off the back of the chair, I spun around and dragged the straps of my dress up my arms. There was a hoarse shout and then the sound of the door unlocking from the outside was like cannon fire in the room.

Damn it. I hadn't planned on anyone coming in this quickly. I needed time to—

The door swung open, and terror poured into my chest as I saw who filled the entirety of the doorway. It was….

It was *the* Prince.

Chapter 4

The fae didn't scare me anymore, not like they used to, but this one… this one terrified and enthralled me in ways I couldn't understand. Ways in which I really didn't even want to try to figure out.

Air lodged in my throat as his gaze immediately zeroed in on me, and I didn't need to pretend to be entranced. I was frozen, rooted to the chair by invisible vines.

I hadn't seen him in what felt like forever, and I wasn't even sure that I had seen him at the hospital after the attack or if that was some kind of bizarre hallucination. I'd been on a lot of powerful drugs. I didn't even know he was still in New Orleans. I'd figured he'd gone to Florida, to the community his brother oversaw.

The Prince was what was called an Ancient, fae that had lived for hundreds of years, if not more, and were not only capable of a hell of lot more than a normal fae was, but they were nearly impossible to kill. Stabbing them with iron did absolutely nothing beyond pissing them off. You couldn't send them back to the Otherworld. You had to kill them, and that was only accomplished by separating the head from the body.

And good luck with that.

Ancients were the most powerful of the fae and they could be Knights or Princesses or Princes or Queens.

Or a King.

They didn't look like a fae. Their skin wasn't silvery and the point to their ears was hardly noticeable, which enabled them to blend in with humans and escape the Order's detection until it was too late.

He was supposed to be good, so why in the hell was he here, at

Flux, in a club frequented by the enemy—*his* enemy?

The Prince cocked his golden head to the side while my heart threw itself against my ribs. Did he recognize me? There was no way. I was well disguised, even beyond the wig. I'd discovered that I had a flair for makeup. I basically reshaped the features of my face with contouring and a keen eye and steady hand.

He couldn't know it was me, because it wasn't like he'd paid attention to me. It wasn't like *anyone* paid attention to me. I was a ghost in most rooms, unseen even when I wanted to be seen and heard. That was one thing that hadn't changed after the attack. And it was freaking ironic that the one thing I hated the most about myself, how easily I took to just blending in, had become my greatest asset.

I willed my heart to slow, but when he closed the door behind him, my heart launched into my throat. He was supposed to be good, but he was *here*, and if it came down to fighting, there was a slim chance I'd win.

Or land a single kick.

"You're alone." His voice… God, his voice was deep and melodious, an odd accent that reminded me of twinkling lights and lush flowers. "Are you alone?" he repeated.

I let the façade of being entranced slip over me and murmured, "Yes?"

"Is that so?" He strode forward, coming closer, into the dim light offered by the exposed lightbulb screwed into a ceiling fan. The Prince was…. God, he was strikingly beautiful.

Golden blond hair brushed broad shoulders and framed high, sharp as a blade cheekbones and a jaw that could've been carved out of marble. His brow was several shades darker than his hair and his nose straight, aristocratic. Full, expressive lips were currently pressed together in a hard line. There was no glamour to fade away. This was what he looked like, an example of inhuman perfection designed to lure the prey in.

My pulse pounded as I kept my gaze level.

"You were in here with someone."

Oh God, there was a good chance I was going to vomit. Just a little. In my mouth.

"Where did he go?" He was now in front of me, standing a few feet away.

"I… I don't know?" I said it like it was a question, like I knew humans under a trance would speak.

"Really?" His voice dripped with derision.

A fine sheen of sweat broke out along my skin. Not for one second did he sound like he believed me, so I didn't answer. I stared at his stomach and chest—his rather defined chest that stretched the black thermal he wore.

"Look at me." His voice was a crack of thunder, and I felt like I was tranced.

I lifted my gaze, and I immediately wished I hadn't. I was no short woman, but even if I wasn't sitting down, he would've towered over me. The Prince was around six and a half feet and every inch of him was intimidating. To meet his gaze, I had to tilt my head waaay back.

His eyes.... They were the palest blue color that was startling against the blackness of the pupil and the thick, heavy fringe of his lashes. Only a fae had eyes like that.

Something flickered over his face, gone too quickly for me to figure it out. "What is your name?"

"Sally," I rasped out, throat dry.

"Is it? That's... odd."

One of two things was going to happen at this point if he recognized me. Either he wasn't on Team Good Fae and he was most definitely going to kill me, because there was no way I was going to win a fight with a Prince. That would... suck. Or he was going to haul my ass out of here, report what I was doing to the Order, and then everything would be over. I couldn't allow that to happen either. Not when I was so close to finding the last two fae. So close to complete retribution.

His hand snaked out faster than my eyes could track. Warm fingers folded around my forearm, sending a jolt traveling up my arm, much like the static charge I got from dragging my feet over a carpet. He eyed the bracelets with a sardonic twist of his lips. Would the Prince recognize what they were? I wasn't sure.

Then his gaze lifted to mine as he folded two fingers under my chin, guiding my head farther back. A sound rumbled from him, reminding me of a very animalistic growl. My stomach hollowed. A long, tense moment passed and then he pulled his fingers away from my chin.

"So, Sally, I am confident that you entered a room with someone I am looking for." His thumb slipped over the skin just below the cuff I wore. "Those outside told me he was in here." He paused. "Then again, those outside this room are unable to tell me anything else."

What did that mean?

I thought about the odd thump against the wall. Had he done something to the fae out there?

"He was in here and now he's not." The thumb moved in a slow circle along my skin, causing a tight, confusing shiver to hit me. "Now, what could've happened to this fae? There's only one small window behind you, but I doubt he'd be able to climb out of that. So, it appears as if he… disappeared into thin air."

Well, that did kind of happen.

"I'm rather disappointed, as there were things I needed to discuss with him."

I wanted so badly to ask why the *reformed* Summer Prince needed to talk to a Winter fae.

His hand slid up my hand, so now his thumb was tracing idle, slow circles on the inside of my elbow, just below another scarred bite mark. A mark Tobias could've noticed if he hadn't been so arrogant and stupid.

"Sally, Sally…. What am I going to do with you?" he mused as thick lashes lowered, shielding pale, wolf eyes.

That was… that was a really bad question. And why was he touching me like this, coming so close to the bracelet? And why was it making me shiver instead of making me want to scrape the skin off that he was touching?

I was going to blame his unexpected appearance for my reaction.

When I didn't answer, one side of his lips kicked up in a mockery of a smile. "Stand."

Having no idea if he really believed I was entranced, a tremble coursed through me as I stood on locked knees. The change in position was a blessing. I wasn't looking at his eyes anymore. My gaze was level with his chest.

"Where are you from, Sally?"

The question caught me off guard and it took a moment to answer. "Lafayette," I threw out, figuring my accent betrayed that I was from somewhere south.

"Lafayette?" His other hand landed softly on my waist, and my entire body jolted.

Damn it.

A human entranced would have no reaction. He had to know I was faking this, but that didn't mean that he knew who I was. I couldn't imagine that he did, not when he'd only seen me twice, and both times I hadn't looked like this.

Another tremble coursed through me, and I knew he could feel it, because his grip on my waist tightened, bunching the material of my dress.

"Well, Sally from Lafayette, there's something very interesting about you," he said, and a stuttered heartbeat later, the entire front of my body was pressed against his.

The contact was a shock to my system, and when I drew in a deep breath, he smelled like summer thunderstorms and reminded me of glistening beaches. My skin burned and tingled and the reaction was swift, potent. His hand slid to the center of my back, and the next breath I took caught in my throat.

What in the world was happening? Was he—?

"Your pulse...." His hand followed my spine, tangling in the strands of hair as it curled around the nape of my neck. His warm breath danced over my forehead as he tipped my head back, pressing his thumb right against my wildly beating pulse.

Without warning, he spun me around. My heart skipped a beat as he hauled me back against him. I drew in a ragged breath, fully aware of how my body fitted against the hard slabs of his muscles and the...*holy crap*, the other thing that seemed equally proportioned to his large body, and I desperately wanted to pretend I didn't feel that.

And I also desperately wanted to pretend I didn't feel how my stomach twisted in a pleasant, confusing way or how liquid heat pooled low. I wasn't attracted to him. No way. No way at all, because behind the raw heat building inside me was also fear.

The Prince brushed the heavy hair off the back of my neck and then his fingers were against the taut muscles, working to soothe the tightness there.

What in the hell was he up to?

I'd never had a neck massage before. Honestly, I kind of hated random people touching me, but this was… this was oh so nice. Against my will, my neck arched into his hand as the warming in my stomach spread low, really low. My body seemed to relax and tense all at the same time.

I needed to stop this. Right now.

My eyes drifted shut as his hand made its way from my neck,

skimming down the side of my body, over my lax arm. The tips of his fingers coasted over mine, and then found their way to my hip. A pumping pulse picked up in several key points in my body, responding to the light, forbidden touch.

He didn't speak as his warm breath kissed the curve of my cheek and I didn't say or do anything. I could stop him. I knew I could. Or I could at least try.

I did nothing.

His hand slipped over my stomach, below my navel. I jerked, bringing us closer. Way too close once more, and I couldn't breathe as something bizarre happened inside me. It was like all my senses woke up at once, sparking with life and flaming heat through my veins.

His hand dropped to the front of my dress, right above where a deep, deep ache had started. He growled deep in his throat as he said against the flushed skin of my neck, "Your pulse is racing so fast—too fast for someone entranced."

Hell.

Oh hell.

The Prince might not recognize who I was, but he knew I wasn't entranced. Fight or flight response kicked in, overriding the confusing heat pumping through my body.

Two years ago, I would've chosen flight. That was all I'd been capable of. Not anymore. A whole different instinct took over, a newly developed one. I had no idea why the Prince was here, in the pit of his enemies, and I wasn't willing to risk finding out or being caught by him.

Spinning around, I gripped his forearm as I ducked and twisted, slipping free of his grip. I saw the flicker of surprise on his face and then I spun back toward him. Still holding onto his arm, I used his weight as an anchor as I leaned back. Planting my left leg back, I lifted my right and slammed my knee into his midsection.

The Prince grunted as he let go, but he did not move even an inch. That kind of kick would've brought a human down. Probably would've even knocked a normal fae back several steps, but not an Ancient. He lifted his chin, eyes narrowed with annoyance.

"That was unnecessarily violent," he said, straightening to his full height.

He hadn't seen unnecessarily violent yet.

I spun, picking up the chair. It was surprisingly heavy. Grunting, I swung it around, prepared to at least knock him once upside the head.

Wouldn't kill him, but would definitely give me a chance to escape without having to answer questions.

The Prince's speed was mind-numbingly fast.

I didn't even see him lift a hand. He just suddenly had ahold of the leg of the chair. He wrenched it from my grip, tossing it aside. The chair hit the wall with a bang, shattering into three large pieces.

Damn.

He tilted his head, lips pressed into a hard, flat line. "I'm going to chalk that up to one bad life choice fueled by fear and a little bit of stupidity, and logically reason that you're—"

Spinning into him, I swung my arm out. He dipped to the left, causing my elbow to glance off his chest. Cursing under his breath, he shot toward me. Before I could even take a breath, he had both hands on my shoulders. My back hit the wall, and then he was there, his large body crowding mine in. Panic began to blossom, but I fought it down. I started to raise my leg, aiming for where it counted, but he pressed his hips in, trapping a large thigh between mine.

"Foolish. So very foolish," he said. "Also kind of hot."

Wait. What?

"But that's neither here nor there." He wrapped his hand around my chin, forcing my head back against the wall. His gaze snagged mine. "Are you out of your mind? Do you know how easy it would be for me to kill you? Do you?"

Heart thundering in my chest, I kept my mouth shut as I glared back at him.

"Do you?" he repeated, his eyes churning with anger and… and something… something else. "Answer me."

"Yes," I spat out.

"And you still tried to attack me?" His thumb sliced over my chin. "When I made no move to harm you."

I wouldn't exactly say he made no move. He had grabbed me. That I didn't appreciate.

"I think I can guess what happened to Tobias."

My jaw ached from how tight I was clamping it shut.

Fury poured off him, but when those heavy lashes lowered, I swore his gaze had zeroed in on my mouth. He cursed again, and then suddenly released me. I wasn't expecting him to do it. Off balance, I stumbled forward. He caught my arm, straightening me, and then dropped his hold as if my skin burned him.

"Go," he growled out. "Go before I do something we both will end up regretting."

I didn't need to be told twice.

Backing away from the Prince, I spun on the sharp heel of my boot and then I ran.

Chapter 5

The beautiful antebellum style home I grew up in sat nestled in the middle of the Garden District. With its wraparound porch, second-floor balcony, and the courtyard Mom and I had spent many sunny afternoons in, it was one of the houses that was an utter blast from the past—with the exception of the kitchen and bathrooms that had been renovated about five years ago.

There were days when I thought about selling it and moving on to anywhere but here even though I had been born in this home and New Orleans was a part of my blood just as much as the Order was. If I did decide to sell, I knew this home wouldn't last a second on the market, but I couldn't bring myself to let go of it. At least not yet, when I could still recall all those good memories.

But on nights like tonight, when I was rattled and exhausted as I unlocked the door my mom had decided to paint blue, I was swamped with the bad memories.

The attack had happened less than two blocks from here. We'd been so close to making it back, and I had to think that would've made a difference. Tink had been here.

Then again, if I hadn't panicked and had fought back instead of flailing like a pinned insect, that could've also made a difference.

Swallowing down the bitter ball of emotion, I opened the door and stepped inside, locking it behind me. A lamp on the entryway table was on, casting a soft glow to the formal sitting room to the right—a room that legit was never used, and a cherry oak library to the left. I could hear some sort of conversation coming from the living area at the back of the house, on the other side of the kitchen.

I dropped the keys on the table and strode past the staircase, the heels of what I liked to refer to as my stripper boots clacking off the wood floors as I entered the dining room, another place in the house that saw little use. The kitchen was quiet, the under cabinet lights on, shining down on the gray and white quartz countertops.

Stepping under a rounded archway, I took in the living area at the back of the house. One entire wall was nothing but windows that overlooked the porch and courtyard. The blinds were drawn and the heavy, ceramic lamp was lit. On the screen, my favorite *Stranger Things* kid Dustin was currently trying to lure a baby demogorgon into the basement. There was an enormous bowl of Lucky Charms on the round coffee table. I knew this because the empty box was sitting next to the bowl. No milk. And it looked like all the colorful marshmallows had been picked out of the cereal.

Again.

I sighed as I counted the cans of open soda. Four. How anything could consume that much sugar and not slip into a diabetic coma, I had no idea.

Twisting at the waist, I scanned the normal hiding places. Behind pillows. Under the coffee table. Waiting behind the end tables. The room was empty.

Picking up the remote, I turned the television off and then I grabbed the bowl of cereal. I brought it back to the kitchen and placed it on the counter before returning to grab the empty soda cans. I tossed them into the recycling bin, all the while not thinking about what I'd done tonight or the Prince or how sore my throat was. Once I was done cleaning up, I went through the narrow hall that was lined with framed photographs of Mom and me, and older ones of my father. Back to the foyer, I double-checked the locked door.

Couldn't be too safe.

As I wearily climbed the stairs, I spotted a tiny shoe no bigger than half my pinky sitting between two wooden spindles on the steps. Stopping, I looked for the other shoe, but didn't see it and decided to leave that shoe on the step, because I figured it was there for a reason.

The upstairs hallway light was already on, so I turned it off as I reached the end of the hall and then closed the bedroom door behind me.

Feeling several years older than my age, I crossed the quiet room and walked into what used to be a small nursery, but had been converted into a walk-in closet ages ago.

Then I started my routine of becoming me again—becoming Brighton Jussier.

I bent down and got to unzipping the boots. Kicking them off, I reached up and moved my fingers through the hair, finding the extra bobby pins I used as an extra precaution. I plucked them out, dropping them in a glass tray sitting on the waist-high table in the center. Slipping the wig off, I placed it on the plastic mannequin-head stand and then peeled off the cap that helped keep my hair flat. I had no idea how to braid, so I worked with a low bun. After another half a dozen pins joined the rest in the tray, my hair was free, falling past my shoulders. A rush of blood hit my scalp and I closed my eyes, enjoying the tingles.

Lifting my hands, I looked up as I pinched my fingers, removing the contacts that had changed my eyes to blue. I placed them in their container.

The dress came off next, going straight into the trash. I never wore them twice. I just couldn't bring myself to do it, because even though this one was sparkly and sexy, it would forever make me think of Tobias and his icy touch. It would always remind me of the first time I saw him and why I had hunted him down.

Undressed, I tugged on the fluffy robe and then padded barefoot back across the room to the bathroom.

I turned on the shower, letting the steam begin to fill the space. It took two towelettes to remove all the makeup on my face, but after a handful of moments, it was *my* face staring back at me in the mirror.

Blonde hair fell limply around cheeks that were pink from all the scrubbing. Faint shadows clung to the skin under eyes that reminded me of my mother. They were wide-set and brown. Someone once called them doe eyes, and I think they might've been suggesting that my eyes gave them the impression of a deer in headlights. Right now, that would be accurate. I stared at myself like I didn't recognize anything about my own face. My gaze lowered, to where my lips were slightly parted and then lower still.

Pale blue marks had formed on either side of my throat.

Without having to try, I heard the sound the Prince had made when he'd tipped my head back. Smoothing my fingers over the faint bruises, I wondered if the Prince had seen them. Was that why he'd... growled?

What in the hell was the Prince even doing at Flux?

And I couldn't help but wonder why he hadn't struck back at me.

He could've. I'd kicked him. Swung a chair at him. Hit him, and all he did was restrain me and then told me to leave. He'd been pissed, that much I was sure of, but he didn't try to hurt me.

Steam crept across the mirror, blurring my reflection as I pulled my hand away from my throat. When I'd left the room, there hadn't been a single fae in the alcove on the second floor. The couches and chairs were empty. There wasn't even a human in sight. The Prince had done something to the fae.

I didn't think he'd warned them off.

He'd taken them out, and that made sense. The fae that frequented Flux were the Winter fae, the enemy of the Summer Court and humans, but what didn't make sense was why he was looking for Tobias.

I knew why I'd been there. Just like I knew I would go back to Flux, because eventually the remaining two fae would make an appearance. They always did, and I would do the same thing I'd done tonight. Watch them. Learn their habits. Strike fast and get out, hopefully without The Prince showing up. I would kill them or die trying, and there was a good chance that would happen, because one of the two remaining fae was an Ancient.

And he'd been the cruelest, the sickest.

I shuddered as I gripped the sink. Closing my eyes, I inhaled deeply and then held my breath a second before the all-too-familiar thought blasted forward, shoving everything else out of the way.

This isn't who you are.

Stalking the fae and putting myself in ridiculously dangerous positions wasn't who I used to be. That was who I'd wanted to be, but what I had become was some kind of twisted version of that.

Being consumed with vengeance was something I never thought I'd experience, but I was knee-deep in it and I wasn't coming out anytime soon.

Who I used to be was a woman I could barely remember. I'd once thought that my life had changed when I was twelve and that my life could never be that rattled again. I'd foolishly believed that every human had a cap to what kind of tragedy they'd experience, and I'd already had my fair share. My father had died in the line of duty, as many Order members did, before I could even form one memory of the man. My mom had been brutalized but survived to never be a hundred percent the same again. I'd watched friends die in the battle against the fae, and naïvely, stupidly thought that we were free and clear, because how could anything else happen to me or my mother? We'd experienced enough tragedy to last a lifetime. God couldn't be that cruel to deliver yet another soul-crushing blow.

I'd been so wrong.

Thinking back to the night of the attack, I wondered if I had misjudged the reason for Mom being antsy. Maybe it wasn't a sign that she was about to have another episode. Maybe it was some kind of primal instinct had told her what was coming that night. What if she had known that those were the last hours of her life?

Guilt churned, flooding the pit of my stomach with acid as I walked myself back through the night. Our shouts of surprise and screams of pain had been quickly silenced. They'd swarmed us within seconds, pulling us into the courtyard of the empty home.

They'd torn through clothing, skin, and muscle. The pain... God, it had been shattering and devastating. They hadn't even attempted to feed on us. I'd learned later from Ivy that Gerry and the others hadn't appeared to have been fed on either. The attack was all about pain and blood, and there'd been so much blood. It had coated my skin and soaked my hair.

I'd fought to stay conscious, but it was all too much. The pain. The blood. The *sounds*. The shock of it all. I wasn't able to hold on, and the last thing I'd felt was my mother's hand slipping from mine. The last thing I'd seen had been her. I'd seen what they had done to her. No human could survive that.

My chest and throat burned until the point I started to feel faint. Dragging in a deep breath of air, I opened my eyes and saw nothing but mist.

Leaning forward, I dragged my hand across the mirror, wiping away the steam until I could see myself staring back at me.

It was my face and my hair. No makeup or special contouring. Those were my lips and my eyes. I was staring at me, but I....

I didn't recognize who I'd become.

Chapter 6

I jolted awake, heart racing and my pulse throbbing in very interesting places as my eyes snapped open. My gaze fixed on the churning ceiling fan. Oh my God, I'd been dreaming.

Not the usual one, reliving the final moments of the fae I'd sent back to the Otherworld, like I normally dreamt after such an event. I'd been back at the club, in that dingy room, but Tobias was nowhere to be seen. I'd been in that same chair, though, and I hadn't been alone.

The Prince had been underneath me.

It had been his warm lips skating down my neck, his hot fingers skating along my sides, and I hadn't been sitting there, holding myself immobile. Oh no, I'd been rocking against him, head thrown back, panting as I moved over him, against him, feeling things I hadn't felt in... in what felt like forever, if *ever*.

I'd woken up right when his fingers had found the clasp of my bra, and there was a tiny, stupid and utterly insane part of me that was now staring at the ceiling fan, disappointed.

Good God, I needed help.

Lots of mental help.

A soft purring sound drew my attention as I willed my heart to slow down and my body to get back on the sane and safe path. I turned my head to the right and found myself eye to eye with two yellow eyes.

Meow.

I frowned as the all gray cat—except for its tail, which looked like it had been dipped in white paint—stretched out his little legs and yawned right in my face.

"How did you get in here, Dixon?" I asked the cat, which was named after a character on The Walking Dead. Dixon didn't belong to me, but he was kind of a package deal at the moment. Not that I minded. I liked the little guy.

Dixon flopped on his side and twisted his head so he was staring at me upside down. I raised a brow and then heard a soft creaking noise. I rose onto my elbows. The iPad slipped off my chest and fell to the floor, the soft thump drawing a sigh from me. I'd fallen asleep... putting a jigsaw puzzle together.

Again.

Kind of lame, but it always relaxed me, helping shut my brain down so I could sleep, but I really needed to stop falling asleep mid-puzzle like a narcoleptic.

I scanned the large dimly-lit bedroom, but the buttery glow from the bedside lamp only held the shadows back from the bed. The thin slice of slivery moonlight seeping through between the curtains did very little to cut through the darkness, but I was confident no one was—

A lump formed under the thin bedspread near the foot of the bed, about the size of a crab. A really *large* crab.

What in the holy hell?

I watched the lump work its way up the bed, stop every couple of inches, and then start moving again. I waited until it was near the top and then leaned over, gripping the bedspread and ripping it back.

The *crab* let out a surprised shriek as I revealed the actual owner of the cat. Tink was... well, he was not of this world. Obviously. He was a brownie, a creature that stood about twelve inches tall, had a major addiction to sugar, TV and film, and Amazon Prime. He'd gotten trapped in this world several years ago while trying to close one of the doorways to the Otherworld. Ivy had found him in St. Louis Cemetery with a broken leg and wing. Instead of putting him down, like all members of the Order were required to do at the time, she'd felt bad for the little guy and taken him home, helping him recover.

What Ivy hadn't known was how crazy powerful Tink was, and that his current state, when he was about the size of a Ken doll, was a size he *chose* to be. Tink was what I liked to call giant-sized when he wanted to be. Ever since he'd come to stay with me, he'd been this size. Why, I had no idea.

Tink used to freak me out. I like to think a flying brownie would freak any normal person out, especially because he was the only brownie ever to be seen in our world. But not only had he grown on me, he was the reason I hadn't bled out on the sidewalk alongside my mom the night I was attacked.

It had been Tink—full-sized Tink—who had found us.

And since then, since I returned home from the hospital, it was like I suddenly had joint custody of Tink. Not that Ivy or I really had custody of him, but he spent the same amount of time with me as he did with her nowadays.

"What are you doing, Tink?" I asked.

The brownie was still flat on his stomach, mid-military crawl. One gossamer wing twitched. Vibrant blue eyes were wide and blond hair a spiky mess. "Hi?"

I narrowed my eyes. "Tink."

He sighed heavily, as if I was the one who had disturbed him, and pushed up on his small arms. He rose onto his knees. "I woke up."

"Okay."

"And I was bored."

"All right."

"Then I went downstairs to finish watching Stranger Things, but someone turned the TV off. Not going to name names or anything—"

"You know it was me, and you could've turned the TV back on." I didn't even bother pointing out that I knew he'd watched both seasons at least eight times. If I did, it would've started a conversation about how he was comparing the upside down to the Otherworld, and I really wasn't in the mood for that conversation at the moment.

"I could've, but then I was like, that requires effort. You have no idea how long it takes these little legs to get down all those steps."

"Couldn't you just fly?"

"That's a lot of work."

"Couldn't you just become people-sized?"

He cocked his head to the side. "But I'm cuter like this."

All I could do was stare at him.

Tink stood and started stomping up the bed, toward Dixon. "So, anyway, then I was like, I wonder what Brighton is doing."

I didn't even want to know what time it was, but I figured it was either really late or really early. "Sleeping, Tink. That's what I was doing."

"But your light was on." He lifted his hand, and Dixon reached out with a paw the size of his head. "So, I thought you were up. Dixon and I decided to visit you, because we're good friends like that."

Sighing, I lay back down.

"Guess what?"

"What?" I asked, scrubbing my hands over my eyes.

"I rode Dixon in here, like I would ride a mighty steer charging into battle."

Lifting my hands, I looked over at him. I really had nothing to say to that.

Tink flashed straight, sharp teeth. "Ivy always gets mad at me when I do that, but Dixon likes it and I like it."

"The world is your oyster, Tink."

"Any-who-boo, we waited up for you." He caught Dixon's paw with both hands and shook it. "You were late. Super late. So, we went to bed."

"You don't have to wait up for me. I told you that." I rolled onto my side, facing him. Tink was still shaking Dixon's paw. For the hundredth time since he showed up at my doorstep a week ago with Dixon in tow, I wondered why he was still here and not in Florida. "Can I ask you something?"

"You can ask me anything, Light-Bright."

I grinned at the ridiculous name. "Why didn't you go to Florida with Ivy?"

"Because she was with Ren." He rolled his eyes.

"You like Ren. Don't play."

"He's *tolerable*."

I searched his face. "And Fabian went down to Florida. Wouldn't you want to be with him?"

"I went down to Florida with him last September, and I decided after thorough exploration that Florida is the Australia of the United States. The place scares me," he said, and I snorted at that, because it was sort of true. "He's not going to be down there forever. He's coming back."

I wondered if there was something wrong between him and Fabian. "Is everything okay with you guys?"

"Of course." Tink dropped Dixon's paw and pinned me with a look that said he couldn't believe I'd actually asked that question. "Fabian not only thinks that I'm the most amazing creature to walk this world and beyond, he's so in love with me, it's adorable."

My grin grew as I reached over and scratched Dixon behind the ear. "That's good."

"Speaking of love, how was your date?" He changed the subject as he plopped down on the pillow beside mine and crossed his legs, leaning back against Dixon's fluffy belly.

"Date?" I almost laughed right in Tink's face. As if I ever had a date. Kind of hard meeting people when you were a member of the Order, knew that fae existed outside of Disney and fairytales, had a twelve-inch brownie who sometimes was people sized and often crawled into my bed when he was Tink sized—*wait*. His brows lifted. "Oh, it wasn't that good. Nothing to write home about."

Tink folded his arms. "You lied to me. You didn't have a date."

"I—"

"You went hunting instead, didn't you?" His little mouth pursed with irritation. "You went hunting for one of those fae who hurt you, but you didn't want me—the most awesome of awesome company to ever be blessed with—to tag along."

"Tink—"

"Not only am I freaking awesome, I am also pretty damn badass. If you go out there hunting those fae, you take me with you. I can help."

"Tink—" I tried again, no point in lying. He knew what I was doing. He was the only one to figure it out. "I know you're awesome company, but the moment they saw you, they'd know what you were. That would kind of throw a wrench into everything."

"Oh, yeah, and you ending up dead or worse would also throw a wrench into everything." Tink leaned away from Dixon. "What you're doing is dangerous. If Ivy knew—"

"Ivy's not going to know. Neither is Ren or anyone else," I told him. "Look, I get that you're concerned, but I don't want you out there, putting yourself at risk. You've already done so much," I told him, meaning it. "You saved my life."

Tink shook his little head as he stared at me, gaze somber. "I didn't save your life. I found you. That's all I did."

"You still saved me."

"No," he said, louder this time. "It wasn't me who saved you."

I opened my mouth, unsure of what to say. The way he said that struck me as odd, but before I could say anything, he spoke again.

"Did you find who you were looking for?"

"Yes."

"Did you take him out?" Tink asked, holding my gaze.

"Yes," I whispered.

Tink smiled then. "Good."

Chapter 7

Miles, the leader of the New Orleans branch of the Order, called first thing Monday morning with a request that both confused and interested me.

The Summer fae had requested a meeting with the Order, but Miles couldn't spare any of the *essential* members to go see what they wanted.

Since I was not considered an essential Order member, I'd been assigned the task to figure out what they could possibly want.

Tink was passed out in the living room next to Dixon, so I didn't bring him along with me. Granted, I could've woken him up, but the fae treated Tink like he was some kind of golden calf to be worshipped, and Tink's head was already overinflated, adorably so.

So, that's where I found myself Monday morning, staring at the beam of sunlight that shone through the large windows of the office inside Hotel Good Fae, keeping the room nice and toasty despite the chilly March temperatures outside.

That's what Ivy called this place, and it did remind me of a hotel—a really glitzy, mammoth hotel. To humans and even to the Winter fae, Hotel Good Fae appeared to be nothing more than an abandoned power plant on St. Peters Street.

Based on the old maps I'd found in my mother's past research clutter, I suspected all the strange markings of places that couldn't or shouldn't exist were more well-hidden communities.

This might not be the only one.

Hotel Good Fae was a massive structure set up a lot like a hotel. Several stories tall with hundreds of rooms on each floor and sprawling communal areas outfitted with multiple cafeterias, theaters, shopping, gyms, and even space for a school of sorts, the compound had the ability to house thousands of fae. The Order had no idea exactly how many fae lived in this place, something that I knew disturbed Miles and the other Order members.

The kind of power and magic the Summer fae used to glamour the building was astonishing.

It was a good thing they didn't want to feed off humans and seemed to like us, because if not, we'd be so screwed.

Then again, I knew that Prince Fabian fed, supposedly on willing humans who knew what he was, because he didn't age and was capable of extraordinary actions. I assumed that his brother, *the* Prince, fed too.

Tugging on the neck of my chunky cable-knit sweater, I was beginning to think I would melt in this office before anyone showed up. The sweater had been perfect for when I was outside and it covered the bruises on my neck, but now I was sweltering in it.

If Ivy hadn't been in Florida with her husband handling some kind of super-secret mission, she'd be here, sitting in the Hotel Good Fae, acting as the liaison between the Order and the fae. Not me. She was better at handling these types of meetings, and right now, the best needed to here, because things between the Summer fae and the Order were tense.

I found myself staring at the long, narrow desk in front of me as I waited, smoothing a blonde strand of hair back into the ponytail. The surface was free of clutter. Just a large desk calendar and computer monitor. An iMac. My desk at home looked like maps and books had thrown up all over it. I couldn't even see the top of my desk, let alone use the keyboard to what was definitely not an iMac.

I used one of the guest rooms upstairs for my office, which was perfect, because I could close the door on the room and pretend that a hoarder didn't live there.

Nervous energy filled me as I dropped my hand and ran my fingers along the neck of the sweater. My throat was still tender and I knew it probably would be for a couple of days. At least the weather was cool enough to wear a turtleneck.

Got to look on the bright side.

Pressing my lips together, I dragged my gaze from the empty desk just as I heard footsteps outside the room. I dropped my hand. Seconds later, the door opened.

The Summer fae known as Tanner strode into his office. His real name was totally unpronounceable, as were the names of most of the fae who lived here. Almost all of them, including the woman behind him, had adopted human sounding names. Even the Winter fae did that, because I doubted Tobias had been that bastard's real name.

Tanner drew up short when he spotted me sitting there, as did the female fae called Faye, who was carrying a file. Odd reaction considering when they saw me, I looked like I normally did, no wig or heavy makeup. No façade.

I was Brighton today even if I... I didn't feel like her.

I only saw the mask Faye and Tanner wore for a second before the humanity seeped away and I saw them in all their fae glory. The only thing that hadn't changed was their hair. Both were dark haired, but Tanner's was salt and peppered, proving that he was aging like a human while Faye was younger, her hair a deep flaxen color.

"Ms. Jussier." Surprise colored Tanner's tone as he crossed the room and stopped in front of me, offering his hand. "I am surprised to see you."

"Brighton," I corrected him as I glanced at his outstretched hand. The moment of hesitation didn't go unnoticed by Faye. The shrewd female cocked a dark eyebrow. I took Tanner's hand, shaking it as firmly as humanly possible. I didn't even know why I hesitated other than just being weird—and I was weird. A lot. "You know you can call me Brighton."

He squeezed my hand affectionately. "Goodness, Brighton, I haven't seen you in ages. I'm... I am so sorry to hear about your mother and for what happened to you."

I couldn't remember the last time I'd been in this office or to Hotel Good Fae, but it was before the attack.

"Merle was an amazing and unique woman," he continued, his tone and pale blue eyes full of genuine sorrow, and I wasn't surprised he said that. He and several of the Summer fae had attended her funeral. "She is greatly missed."

The next breath I took got stuck in my throat. I pulled my hand free, placing it on the velvety arm of the chair I sat in. I opened my mouth, but found that I couldn't speak as sorrow and anger threatened to rise up and smother me. I couldn't let that happen. Not here.

Clearing my throat, I pushed away the messy emotions and focused. "Thank you. My mother enjoyed knowing you."

"She did?" Tanner chuckled as he stepped back from me and

turned to his desk. "Your mother was a hard woman to win over."

"She had… trust issues," I explained, shifting in the chair. "But she trusted you. Both of you."

As crazy as that sounded, it was true. Mom actually liked Tanner. I thought she might've been developing a crush on the fae, which sounded absurd considering what she had been through, but she really did like Tanner.

A faint smile crossed Faye's face. "And we consider that a great honor."

Nodding, I wished that the bitter, razor edged ball of emotion that now sat heavily on my chest would just go away. It was time to get this meeting underway. "I can tell you weren't expecting me. Ivy was unable to make it. She's with—"

"Prince Fabian in Florida," Faye finished, standing a few feet from me beside the end of the desk. "We are aware that Ivy isn't available, but we thought they'd send… someone else."

I wasn't sure how to respond to that. I kept my face blank as Tanner sat behind the desk. "I'm sorry, but Miles is busy with the new recruits."

"I imagine he does have a lot on his hands." Tanner smiled, and he was always smiling politely. It was like his face was permanently fixed that way. "But we expected someone… higher up."

Heat crept into my cheeks as my hand on the chair became rigid. *They knew.* I glanced between the two fae, feeling the warmth travel down my throat. They knew that Miles had sent me in for the meeting, because, in all honestly, he was too busy to deal with Tanner and, at the end of the day, didn't really care enough to pull any of the members off the street or out of training. That was why I'd been sent in, because in Miles's eyes, I had disposable time.

I wasn't remotely essential.

I lifted my chin. "I can assure you that I, like every other Order member, has been born and raised within the organization. In reality, I'm more knowledgeable about anything that has to do with the Order than Miles." I wasn't being a braggy-mc-bragster either. That was the damn truth. That was my job at the Order. The researcher. The reader. The studier. I was the *Willow* in an army of *Buffys* and *Angels*. "I can assist you with whatever it is that you need to speak with us about."

"I'm sorry," Tanner was quick to reply. "I didn't mean to insinuate that you couldn't handle this. It's just that…."

"What?" I lifted my brows, waiting.

"You're uncomfortable around us," Faye stated plainly. "Which I can completely understand with what happened to you—"

"What happened to me is irrelevant."

Faye's gaze softened just a little. "I can smell your anxiety. It reminds me of woodsmoke."

Now my face was on fire. Was it truly that obvious that I was anxious? "You can smell my anxiety?"

Faye nodded.

Well, that was something I never knew and that was somewhat creepy.

"And you're gripping the chair like it's some kind of lifeline," Faye pointed out. "It's like you've already forgotten that two years ago, we fought beside the Order and pushed the Queen back into the Otherworld."

Tanner tensed at the mention of the Queen. Couldn't blame him. I'd never seen the Queen, but from what I heard, she was a whole bucketful of nightmares.

"That we lost many good fae that night," Faye continued. "And it seems you've also forgotten that the biggest betrayal did not come from us, but came from within the Order."

"I haven't forgotten." How in the world could I? Betrayal had come from the top of the Order, starting with David Faustin. He was the head of the New Orleans Sect, keyword being *was*, and his betrayal had spread throughout the Order like a virus, infecting nearly everyone. Those within the Order who hadn't died at the hands of the not-so-friendly fae, the Winter fae, had done so at the hands of those they'd trusted.

I exhaled roughly as I eased my grip off the arm of the chair. "I...." I started to apologize but stopped and decided to be as bluntly honest as Faye. "I was raised to hunt fae and taught that there was no such thing as a good fae. And yes, there were some members of the Order who knew of your existence, but the majority of us didn't know that the Summer Court had escaped into our world after the war with the Winter Court, and were just trying to live their best lives as human. If anyone had suggested two years ago that there were good fae out there, fae who weren't feeding on humans, I would've laughed straight in their face."

Faye's jaw hardened, but I wasn't done. "And you know damn well the Winter fae, those still loyal to the Queen, far outnumber you all.

Two years, Faye. That's all I've had, all many of us had to come to terms with the idea that not all fae are evil incarnate. So, yes, the fae make me uncomfortable. Just as I'm sure we make you uncomfortable."

"Of course some of you make us uncomfortable, considering there are still some Order members who want to kill us," Faye shot back.

"I think what Faye is trying to say this whole time, is that we have a fairly serious issue, and we're worried that your... uncomfortableness may get in the way of helping us resolve this issue." Tanner folded his hands on the desk. "That is all."

Okay. Wow. This was getting awkward. "May I be painfully honest?"

"Of course." Tanner sat back.

"Besides Ivy and Ren, there is not a single member of the Order who isn't uncomfortable around the fae or may be somewhat prejudiced by all their years fighting fae who want nothing more than to enslave mankind and destroy them. Even Ren isn't exactly going to be rolling out the red carpet, and his wife is half-fae," I said, holding their stares. "So, if you're worried that my *uncomfortableness* is going to be an issue, then you are going to have the same problem with any Order member besides Ivy. Either you tell me why you wanted a meeting with the Order or you wait until Ivy gets back. Your call."

"It's not just that we make you nervous." Faye tapped the file on her denim-covered thigh. "It's also that we scare you."

My head snapped in her direction. "You do not scare me."

"Is that so?" she murmured.

"That's so. And just to clarify, the anxiety you're sniffing isn't because of you two. I'm just an anxious person ninety percent of the time. You guys make me uncomfortable, but you do not make me anxious or scared. There's a Mississippi River's worth of difference between the two."

A measure of respect filled Faye's eyes. Not much, but I saw it.

"Well then, we will make do, won't we?" Tanner said.

Slowly, I turned back to him, thinking he sounded like he had as much faith as I did that Tink wouldn't create a mess by the time I got home. "I guess so."

"We needed to speak with the Order because we've been noticing a disturbing trend." Tanner took the file Faye handed to him. "Over the last month, several of our younglings have gone missing, and we fear the Order is involved."

Chapter 8

All right, I wasn't expecting that.

He opened the file, and I could see a glossy colored photograph of a young man—a young fae. "As you know, many members of the Summer Court do not venture outside these walls. It's not something that we prohibit, but many find everything they need provided for them here."

I nodded absently. The fact that most of the Summer fae remained within the hidden, sprawling compound worked perfectly for us. It often meant that the fae we encountered on the streets weren't the friendly neighborhood sort.

"Some of the younglings want to experience the... human world and all it has to offer. It has become a sort of rite of passage in a way." Faye propped a slim hip against the desk. "They always keep their loved ones in the loop and they're never gone too long."

"Four in the last month have not come back," Tanner said grimly. "Their parents and friends have not heard from them and the last we've seen them is when they left."

I took several moments to process this. "When you say younglings, are we talking about children size, teenagers or early twenties?"

"Children size?" murmured Faye, blinking rapidly.

"All four are in their late teens, early twenties," Tanner clarified. "These are their photographs and identification."

Watching Tanner display four photographs along his desk sort of stunned me. I started searching for the right thing to say and ended up giving up as my gaze glanced off what were similar to driver's license photos. "You're sure they're missing?"

"Unless they're here and currently invisible, yes," Faye replied dryly.

"That's not what I meant." I scooted forward, getting a better look at the four young fae. All male. Each one named underneath his smiling photo. They were young, probably early twenties, and handsome. I was willing to wager a bet they were even hotter with the glamour and probably were having the time of their lives in the Quarter. "This is New Orleans. There is a lot of stuff they can get into. Crazy stuff."

"We understand that. Many of our younglings do… have an enjoyable time, but they are always in contact with their loved ones," Tanner stated.

I lifted a brow. "A lot of younger people get caught up in the party scene here. They meet new people—" *And hopefully don't feed on them.* "—and they lose track of time. The city swallows people whole, and I don't mean that in a bad way—" *I sort of do.* "—It often spits them back out, exhausted and ready to make better life choices, like, for example, keeping your parents up to date on your whereabouts."

"Do human children not keep their parents informed of their whereabouts, for days if not weeks?" Tanner asked.

I pressed my lips together to stop myself from laughing, because I could tell that was a genuine question. "Some do, but not nearly enough."

"Human offspring may have a lack of respect and courtesy toward their elders, but our younglings do not." Hardness seeped into Tanner's tone. "Our offspring are not raised that way."

"Pretty sure eons of human parents have said those same exact words."

Faye cocked her head. "Be that as it may, that is not the case with our younglings."

Glancing between the two, I shook my head as I chose my words wisely. They thought… they thought the Order was going to be concerned about missing fae, even fae from the Summer Court? As terrible as it sounded, I knew that the Order could freaking care less. "I'm sorry, but I'm not sure what this has to do with the Order."

Tanner didn't respond immediately. "There is a burgeoning concern that they were… mistakenly targeted by the Order."

Tension crept into my muscles. "Are you suggesting that these young fae are not missing, but were killed by the Order?"

"As I said, it is a burgeoning concern and hopefully, a misguided one," Tanner said slowly. "But there have been incidents in the past two years where innocents were slaughtered."

He was right.

Before the war with the Queen and the reveal of the Summer fae, the Order had been 'kill first and most likely never ask questions'. There had been no such thing as good fae. Things were different now. Complicated. "There are new protocols in place, Tanner. The Order does not blindly dispense justice. Any fae targeted by the Order is monitored now and based on whatever evidence gathered—"

"You and I both know that most Order members operate on the basis that the Summer fae do not interact often, if ever, with the human populace." Faye's pale blue eyes glinted. "They assume that every fae they see on the street is the enemy."

I stiffened. "That is not the case."

"Really?" Faye challenged. "Solomon posed no harm to humans and he was slaughtered."

Solomon was a fae who'd been killed a year ago, having been wrongly identified by one of the newer Order members.

"That was a mistake, a terrible mistake, and I'm sorry that it happened." And I was. I wasn't remotely okay with *any* innocent being killed, fae or human. "But that doesn't mean that is the case with these guys."

"There hasn't been just one mistake," Faye pointed out.

"I know that." There'd been... several mistakes. "And I wish there was something I could say or do to change that, but—"

"But the Order is trying to adapt. We understand that and we also understand that this is a learning period for all of us," Tanner said, ever the diplomat. "We know that many Order members have died with the new protocols in place."

Many had.

Six times more than any Summer fae who had been injured by the Order.

Taking the time out to make sure you were killing the right fae proved to be a wee bit dangerous. We'd lost the upper hand and the element of surprise. By the time we'd figure out if a fae wasn't on Team Human, the fae realized who we were.

The Order had been nearly decimated two years ago, and we hadn't been able to rebuild our numbers.

Which was why Miles was always busy with new recruits.

"Is it possible that these fae chose to go off the grid?" I asked, toying with the neck of my sweater. "Perhaps they don't want to live here. There's a big world out there, and some of them that live here have to be interested in seeing it. Especially since they watch our TV shows and movies, read our books and magazines. As nice as this place is, maybe they wanted to experience the world beyond these walls, this city?"

Tanner stared at me like he hadn't considered that.

Silence crept into the room. Faye shattered it as she reached over, picking up a photo of a dark-haired fae. "This is my younger cousin. His chosen name is Benji. He's been missing for a week, and I can assure you that he would not do that to his mother. Not after his father died two years ago, fighting the Queen."

My stomach twisted as I focused on his picture.

"This is his friend Elliot, who went missing about two weeks ago. Benji had told his mother he was going to look for Elliot," Faye continued. "He disappeared since and we haven't heard from either Elliot or Benji."

"I'm... I'm sorry," I whispered, lifting my gaze to hers. "Truly, I am."

"Then help us," Faye said quietly. "You will help us find my cousin and these young fae if you feel sorry."

"All we want is to know if the Order has any idea what happened to them and if they could possibly keep an eye out for these younglings." Tanner spoke up as Faye looked away, her throat working. "Kalen has been out there, searching for them with no luck."

I jolted at the mention of the fae who'd worked closely with Ivy and Ren. I'd assumed he was with them and Prince Fabian.

"I can help," I said after a moment. "Can I have those photographs?"

Tanner nodded.

"I can check with the members to see if any of them look familiar." I wasn't sure if any of the Order members would fess up if they had anything to do with these fae. They were supposed to, but I was learning in the last two years there was very little consequence for these types of situations. "I can also make sure they keep an eye out for them."

Faye handed over the photo of her cousin to Tanner, and he closed the file. Rising from the desk, he walked it over to me. "We appreciate anything the Order can do."

Nodding, I took the file and stood, hoping that none of the Order members recognized these young men. If they did, it probably meant they'd met a tragic, unfair ending.

The meeting was officially over. Faye and Tanner were quiet as they led me out of the office and down an empty wide hall. Upon entering the building, I'd been escorted through the front and not the amazing courtyard, and it looked like they were leading me to the front once more.

As we neared the cafeteria area, I began to see more fae. Some lingered outside the wide archway, others walked to and fro, in small groups or alone. Most didn't pay any attention to me. Others looked on in curiosity while some stared with outright distrust as we made our way to the grand, brightly lit lobby that truly reminded me of an upscale hotel.

"Please contact me directly, whether or not you have any information," Faye said as we passed several occupied couches and chairs.

"I will." I reached into the pocket of my purse, searching for my phone. From here, I was going to have to Uber it back to headquarters over on St. Phillip Street. I glanced over at Faye, and could see the worry etched into her face. The concern tugged at my heart. Lord knew I had this same kind of wretched experience of living through the disappearance of someone you loved and not knowing what happened to them. The desperation was the worst, the need to do everything and anything to find them, but not knowing if what you were doing was right or would even help.

Faye was experiencing all of that.

Stopping, I reached over and placed a hand on her arm. The contact surprised her as she swung her head toward me. "I'm sure your cousin is fine."

Faye held my gaze. "I hope so. After losing his father…."

A slight frown pulled at my brow as Faye trailed off. She tilted her head slightly as a hush descended over the lobby and then she turned back to where we came from. Out of the corner of my eyes, I saw Tanner turn back as well.

"You should leave now, Brighton," she whispered.

An acute shiver danced over my shoulders and the tiny hairs along the nape of my neck rose as I stared down at her dark, bowed head. *Don't turn around. Keep walking.* That's what I kept telling myself. I was done here, and Faye was right, I should leave now.

But I turned around, because some primal instinct inside me already knew who had arrived. And some insane, disturbed part of me just had to see him.

The Prince had entered his lobby, dressed very much like he had been Saturday night. Dark pants. Dark thermal. He wasn't looking at Tanner or Faye or any of the other fae.

Pale, ancient eyes fixed on mine. *He didn't recognize you.* That's what I kept telling myself as a wave of goosebumps spread along my flesh.

I took a step back. Wrong move. Oh God, total wrong move.

The Prince's eyes narrowed.

Tanner murmured something in his native language, and the Prince spoke. I didn't understand a single word he said, but his voice was deep and booming and yet quiet somehow.

The fae turned to stare at me, because the Prince... the Prince hadn't taken his eyes off me.

My heart hammered in my chest as I opened my mouth to say what, I had no idea, because the words turned to ash on the tip of my tongue as the Prince strolled across the lobby, heading straight for me.

Chapter 9

My first reaction to seeing him was the realization that there was a good chance I was going to have a massive heart attack. Dead before thirty-one, right here in the grandiose lobby of Hotel Good Fae.

Which, I guessed, was only a little bit better than dying alone at home, suffocated by stacks of dusty books and piles of handwritten maps.

My second, and probably the most troubling of reactions, was that rollercoaster dip in my stomach in response to seeing him, followed by an acute wave of shivers that had nothing to do with who he was.

Goodness, he was just... I couldn't find the right words other than he did some really stupid things to my hormones.

Somehow I managed not to go into cardiac arrest or punch myself as he stalked toward me with the graceful prowl of a predator. I was a hundred percent human with absolutely no special abilities, but I could still feel the leashed power rolling off him, filling every nook and cranny of the lobby. It was base survival instinct, I figured, alerting the human mind that they were in the presence of a predator.

He didn't recognize you. I repeated that all the way up to the moment he stopped in front of me. *He doesn't know it was you he had his hands on—*

"What are you doing here?" he demanded.

Throat dry, I blinked once and then twice. "Excuse me?"

His pupils seemed to constrict in response to my voice. "I asked why you were here, Brighton."

Air caught in my throat at the sound of my name. "You know my name?"

The Prince tilted his head to the side and the look that crossed his face made me think he was questioning my intelligence.

Okay, that was a stupid question. But in my defense, other than Saturday night, when I was confident that he had no idea that was me, I'd only seen him twice before, both times brief. And we'd never been introduced. Ever. And I couldn't even be sure that I had seen him in the hospital. That could've been a hallucination. Or a weird dream. Like the dream I had Saturday night, when I'd been in his lap and he'd been—

Oh my God, my eyes widened as I felt heat blast my face. I was so not going to think about that when I was standing in front of him. Because it was weird. Totally weird and stupid, but I swore I could feel the warmth from his hands on my sides and his lips—

Good God, I really needed to stop thinking.

Those pupils seemed to constrict even further as he dipped his chin. I drew in a sharp breath. He was closer now and his scent.... Goodness, it reminded me of lazy summer afternoons. Being so close to him again was like standing next to a heater.

Tanner cleared his throat. "My liege, Ms. Jussier is here on behalf of the Order. She will be helping us with the missing younglings."

"Is that so?" he replied wryly.

My eyes narrowed. "Yes, that is so. Tanner contacted the Order and I was sent to handle the meeting and now since it's over, I'll be on my way." I turned from the Prince to Faye, who was currently staring at me like I'd lost my mind. "I'll be in touch, Faye."

I didn't make it very far.

Actually, I was only able to turn halfway by the time I felt the Prince's warm fingers curled around my left wrist. Like before, the contact of his skin against mine was a jolt to the system. It was almost like he was charged with electricity, but I didn't think that was possible.

"Do you understand how serious it is that these younglings are missing?" he asked, speaking low enough that I didn't think anyone else could hear him.

"Yes." My gaze skittered over his shoulder. We had an audience, a rather large, curious audience. Unnerved, I tried to pull my hand free and failed. "Of course I know it's important."

"But do you care?" Those odd, striking eyes latched onto mine.

A shiver danced over my shoulders. "Yes, I care." Offended that he would even ask that question, I tugged on my arm again, getting nowhere. "Can you let go of me?"

"Why would you care when the entirety of the Order does not?" He didn't let go.

"How do you know they don't?" I fired back even though he was mostly right.

"The fact that you'd have to ask that question makes me doubt your intelligence," he said. "Then again, I already have good enough reasons to doubt that."

My mouth dropped open. Literally. "Did you just say that to me?"

"I am confident that I spoke in your native language and quite clearly."

Anger flashed through my system. "You don't even know me."

"Oh, I know you." His voice dropped even further, eliciting an unwanted, confusing as hell shiver from me. "I know exactly what and who you are."

My fingers curled into a fist. "I don't even know what you're suggesting."

"You know just as well as I do that the Order doesn't give a damn what may or may not have happened to a few Summer fae." As he spoke, the space between us seemed to have evaporated. "And you stand before me, claiming that you do while you won't even admit that the people you work for couldn't care less."

I opened my mouth and then closed it. Damn, he had a point. A good point, but that didn't mean I was apathetic. "I do care. If I didn't, I wouldn't have taken this file. I wouldn't have told Tanner and Faye that I would see what I could find out. If you actually did know who and what I am, whatever the hell that means, you'd know that I wouldn't lie."

Faye's audible sharp inhale warned me that my voice had risen even though the Prince's hadn't, and at least she could hear me.

I didn't care. Frustration and irritation had long since replaced the healthy sense of fear. "And seriously, dude, can you let go of my arm?"

The Prince ignored my request yet again. "You are nothing but lies and façades."

My entire body jerked at that comment, striking too close to home for comfort. "Let go of me."

He held my gaze as he slowly lifted one finger after another, releasing my wrist. That bitter knot was back in my throat. The Prince had let go and his heavy lashes lowered, shielding his powerful gaze, but I swore I could still feel it. "My apologies," he murmured. "That was uncalled for."

A feather could've knocked me over right then. He was apologizing? The Prince? "Yeah, it was." I swallowed hard, taking a step back from him.

"Even if it is true," he added.

"Wow. Way to ruin an apology," I muttered. "Not that you probably even know why you just apologized."

"I do. It hurt you. Those words."

"What? You can smell that, too?"

Those heavy lashes lifted, and the intensity of his gaze pierced me. Suddenly I thought back to the day I woke up in the hospital, to those eyes. "I can sense many things."

Oh.

Oooh.

I had the distinct impression that he was talking about earlier, when I was thinking about the dream I had. And boy, didn't that make me want to crawl up in a hole somewhere. At that moment, I made a mental note to legit not feel anything when I was around him or any other fae.

One eyebrow, several shades darker than his golden hair, lifted.

"Wait. Can you guys read minds?" I asked, voice hushed and thinking I didn't know nearly as much about the fae as I thought I did.

"We don't need to."

Relief hit me, but it quickly faded when his words cycled back through my head. *We don't need to.* Meaning picking up on our emotions probably gave them enough insight on what our thoughts were.

Nice.

"Well..." I held the folder closer to my chest. "That's freaky."

His lips twitched.

"And I need to go." I started to turn once more, ordering myself not to run out of the lobby like it was on fire. But I stopped, facing him again. "I do care about these younglings. I will find them or I will find out what happened to them."

The Prince inclined his head. A moment passed and then he nodded. Thinking this super awkward face to face was now, thankfully, over, I started to turn away again.

"Brighton?"

Desperately ignoring how the way he said my name made me think of stormy summer nights, I faced him, even though common sense screamed that I shouldn't. I just couldn't help myself. It wasn't a compulsion. It was apparently really bad self-control. My wry gaze flickered over his face, and I bit back a sigh. He was the strongest, the deadliest of his kind, and that knowledge did nothing to dampen my appreciation of his masculine beauty.

"The red hair was a nice touch, but I prefer it this way."

And then with those parting words, he turned and stalked off, leaving me standing there knowing one thing only.

The Prince knew it was me Saturday night.

Chapter 10

Damn.

Damn it.

Damn it all to hell.

Faye followed me out into the thick, overcast skies. "That was weird."

"You think?" Shaken, I pulled out my phone and opened the car service app. Thank Mary Mother of God, Faye hadn't heard what the Prince had said before he walked off. "Yeah, that was super weird."

My heart was still pounding like I'd just done an hour on the treadmill. He knew. Damn it, he knew it had been me. He probably also knew why Tobias had disappeared.

I dragged my teeth along my bottom lip as I checked out what cars were nearby, resisting the urge to rip off the damn sweater. It was much cooler out here, but I still felt too hot.

"Brighton?"

Lifting my chin, I glanced at Faye. She stared at me with some sort of wonder in her eyes. "I don't think you understand how out of character that was for him."

"Oh, trust me, I was on the receiving end of all that weirdness. I understand."

She gave a slight shake of her head. "No, you don't. I've never seen him speak to anyone for that length of time."

"Really?" I choked out a laugh as I glanced over my shoulder at the door that now looked like a rusted-over scrap of metal. The glamour had settled into place. "He spoke to me for about a minute, two tops."

Faye nodded back at me.

"Seriously?" I lowered my phone. "That's not very long. Does he not talk?"

"Not really."

"To anyone?"

"No." She folded her arms as she stepped in closer to me. "Not even his brother. He's... well, you know what he's been through."

And I knew what he, under trance, had put others through. But I kept that to myself.

"He's not very communicative," she said.

He didn't seem like he *peopled* very well, but I also kept that to myself and instead let curiosity get the best of me. "Has he been here this whole time? In the city, since the fight with the Queen?"

"Yes." Her dark brows knitted together. "He actually hasn't left New Orleans at all, not even to travel to the other large community in Florida with his brother."

I thought that was odd, that I hadn't seen him, and none of the Order had ever mentioned seeing him while on patrol. But I had a feeling the Prince knew how to stay unseen until he wanted to be.

I wanted to ask her if she knew why he would've been at Flux looking for a Winter fae, but asking that question would expose that I had been there.

Brushing my ponytail over my shoulder, I returned to the app on the phone. I tapped on the nearest car. "I honestly don't know what to say. It was weird, but it's over. I need to get to the Order. They'll have their afternoon meeting soon and that's the perfect time to see if any of them recognize these guys."

"What was he saying to you?" she asked.

I held onto my phone and the file as I turned to the road, wishing the car would magically appear. "Nothing," I said. "Nothing that's important."

Faye didn't respond to that, and she didn't say anything while she stood out there with me until the car arrived and I climbed in. I doubted that she believed me. When I closed the door and looked out the window, she was already gone.

"St. Phillips Street?" the driver asked, checking my request in the app.

"Yes." My gaze was glued to the rundown brick building as the driver turned around and headed back toward the Canal. "Thank you."

Once I could no longer see the building, I fell back in the seat with a sigh. God, what had just happened? Usually no one paid any attention to me on any given day and the Prince, who apparently didn't speak to anyone, knew it had been me Saturday night and I had a sinking suspicion that he'd somehow known I'd been there and sought me out.

I ran my hand under my throat, wincing as I placed too much pressure on the skin. The Prince knew what I was up to, but he hadn't exposed me in front of Tanner and Faye. Did that mean he wouldn't go to the Order?

And what in the hell did he mean by the claim that he knew who and what I was? Those words haunted the short trip back to headquarters.

Thanking the driver, I climbed out and glanced at the first floor Order-owned shop. Mama Lousy sold all kinds of random stuff, featuring a lot of iron amidst an interesting amount of voodoo tools and authentic *N'awlins* spices. It was currently staffed by one of the grouchiest old men I'd ever met. Jerome had retired from the Order well over a decade ago and somehow ended up in the position that made least sense.

He was so not someone who should be in a customer service position.

Honestly, I was surprised Miles hadn't assigned me to the shop. I snorted and then sighed, because I figured that day was coming sooner rather than later.

One glance through the shop windows, I could see him sitting behind the counter, glaring at the tourists who were picking up various masks and trying them on. He didn't see me, and if he did, it wouldn't have helped with his attitude.

Grinning, I headed for the side entrance and threw open the door. I headed up the narrow, cramped hallway that smelled vaguely of sugar and gym sneakers. A small camera was positioned at the top of the stairs. Things had gotten more high tech in the last two years since the headquarters had been breached by the Prince when he was all 'kill, kill everyone'. A sensor was on the door, above the hand. Pressing my finger on it, I waited as the contraption read my fingerprint. The door unlocked in a jiffy, and as soon as I opened it, I saw that I'd made it back just in time.

The main room was full with at least a half dozen Order members. I immediately saw Jackie Jordan. The dark-skinned woman was sitting on a desk, one long, lean leg curled up as she watched something on her phone. Standing next to her was Dylan, decked out in black tactical pants and a fitted black T-shirt. Besides Miles and Ivy and Ren, they were the only original Order members left. The rest were gone, having perished in the battle or afterward, when the Winter fae unleashed their anger at being foiled. Those members were now replaced by various members from other cities or brand spanking new ones.

An unwanted but familiar heaviness settled in my chest. There had been so much loss and there were echoes of it everywhere. In Jackie and Dylan's weary eyes and in all the new faces crowding the main room.

What had happened to my mother and me hadn't been isolated. Dying in battle was a far better death than being hunted down, caught off guard and unprepared, slaughtered before you even knew what was happening.

I glanced down at the file. Were any of them really going to care about these missing younglings when so many of them had lost friends and family while fighting the fae? Would it matter to them that the Summer Court had come through for us and had fought side by side with us?

I had a terrible feeling I already knew the answer to my questions.

Holding the file close to my chest, I ducked my chin. Skirting around the group that was waiting on Miles, I passed several closed doors and then the surveillance room, where I could always find our leader. And there he was, standing before several rows of monitors hooked up to various cameras all across the city in the dimly lit room. He wasn't alone.

Rick Ortiz sat in one of the chairs, his finger clicking away on the mouse, changing the images on the top row of monitors. As I entered the room, he glanced over his shoulder and lifted a dark eyebrow. That was about the only reaction I got from the olive-skinned man that had transferred to NOLA from Houston. He returned to clicking through the video feed.

Drawing in a short, irritated breath, I started to speak.

"How'd the meeting go?" Miles asked.

Did the man have eyes in the back of his head, hidden by the brown hair cropped close to his skull? "It went okay, but rather unexpected."

"How so?"

Stepping forward, I cleared my throat. "Several of the younglings have gone missing. They're worried that they may have met an…

untimely demise at the hands of the Order."

Rick snorted. "Untimely demise?"

"Well, yes." I shifted my weight from one foot to the other. "Untimely because the Summer fae—"

"Are not to be killed, I know." Rick sat back in his chair and spun it around, facing me. The man was handsome, with dark hair and a neat, trimmed beard, but I also liked to refer to him as Rick the Dick, because his handsomeness was outweighed by his douchieness. "But I just find it funny that they call it untimely."

Having no idea why that was funny and deciding I was not going down that rabbit hole with Rick the Dick, I shifted my attention to Miles, who still wasn't looking at me. He was focused on a camera that was across from the haunted LaLaurie House. The feed wasn't set up for that home. Nope. It was for the rather plain, squat two-story home next to it, the location of one of the doorways to the Otherworld. Why was he watching that so intently? Was there activity there? My stomach dropped all the way to my toes.

The Queen could come back. She had the means—a crystal that powered the doorways from the Otherworld. I started to ask, but I didn't get a chance.

Rick the Dick apparently wasn't done. "You know what else I find funny? That they think we care that some of their spawn are missing."

Miles sighed so heavily it could've rattled the monitors.

Taking a deep breath, I counted to ten. "They want to see if perhaps any of the Order members recognize them and to keep an eye out."

"You got photographs of them?" Miles asked.

"Of course—"

"Hang them up on the bulletin board, so everyone can see."

I started to frown. "I was planning to do that, but I thought I could check with them before the meeting gets started—"

"That won't be necessary." Miles faced me then. The man was in his late thirties, possibly early forties, and he'd seen a lot of messed-up stuff, especially after David's betrayal. He was the hardest man to read, and I couldn't remember ever seeing him smile. Not even once. "Hanging up the photographs should be enough."

That wasn't enough. I knew damn well no one ever looked at the bulletin board. There was still a picture of kittens Jackie had been trying to adopt out over a year ago. "Talking with them would only take a minute or so. One of these missing younglings is Faye's cousin," I added, thinking that would get him to agree, since Faye had helped the Order a million times over.

Miles strode over to where I stood and took the file out of my hands. He opened it and thumbed through the photos. "None of them look familiar." He turned to Rick. "What do you think?"

Glancing over them, Rick lifted a shoulder. "Not to me, but they all kind of look the same."

"Really?" I tensed. "Did you really just say that?"

He smirked. "It's the truth."

"No, it's not, and that sounds really—"

"Don't say racist," Rick cut me off. "The fae are not human. They are not people."

"Wow." I started toward where he sat and stopped myself. "They are kind of a race of beings, so the term racist would apply."

"That's not how that works," he replied, grinning that irritating shit-eating grin up at me.

Miles spoke before I could. "Hang up their photographs, Brighton. I'll tell those on patrol to keep an eye out for them." Closing the file, he handed it back to me. "But I'm telling you now, if one of them did come across one of those younglings and it ended badly, ain't none of them going to come forward with that info."

I figured that much, but hearing Miles say it like it was no big deal sent a wave of disappointment through me. "They should. They're not supposed to harm them. If you think they have, shouldn't there be consequences?"

Rick laughed—straight-up laughed.

"What?" I demanded, feeling my cheeks start to warm.

"You don't patrol, honey. You sit behind a desk and you read books and study maps, sometimes you help out in the infirmary and you handle shit that we don't need to know about. If you did patrol, then you'd know that shit happens out on the street and one second of hesitation can get yourself killed. We're not going to punish someone for doing their job."

Heat blasted my face, and I came so close knocking him out of the chair and explaining to him that I knew exactly what happened when you hesitated, but I managed to restrain myself. "First off, don't call me honey, and more importantly, don't sit there and talk to me about how dangerous these streets are. I know better than you do."

He opened his mouth, but I wasn't done. "We're not supposed to harm the Summer fae. End of story. That's not our job and the new protocols—"

Rick scoffed as he lifted his hands. "Fuck the new protocols."

"Do you hear him?" Exasperated, I turned to Miles. "I mean, you're standing right there."

"Thank you both for stating the obvious and speaking as if you are the leader around here," Miles replied dryly. "Hang the pictures, Brighton. And you?" He turned to Rick. "Shut the hell up, Rick, and get out there."

And with that, Miles stalked out of the office, whistling loudly to gain the attention of everyone who waited in the main hall.

I was dismissed without really even being dismissed. How freaking messed-up was that? Not that I should be surprised. Again, to Miles and to everyone here I wasn't *essential*.

Rick rose, brushing my shoulder as he walked past me. He stopped at the doorway and waited until I faced him. "What?"

He studied me a moment. "I don't get it."

"Get what?"

"Why you'd even care about those fucking fae, after what they did to your mother—did to you?"

Nausea twisted up my insides, but I pushed past it. "The Winter fae attacked my mother and me. Not the Summer fae. Not these boys."

"Does that really matter? What court they claim to belong to? Does that make a difference?" he challenged.

"Yes. It does." It *had* to.

Something akin to pity crossed his face. "Whatever. You do realize that hanging their photographs up is pretty pointless, right?"

"Why?" I lowered the file. "Because no one is going to care?"

"Well, yeah, that. But it's pointless because if they're legit missing and one of us does recognize them, they're probably no longer in this realm. They're dead for all intents and purposes."

Chapter 11

I'd copied the photographs and tacked them onto the bulletin board, over Jackie's year-old kittens' poster, even though Rick didn't think it would make a difference. I'd also managed to corner Jackie before she headed out for patrol. She hadn't recognized any of the younglings, and I believed her. Jackie might be old school and not exactly a fan of any fae, but she wasn't a liar.

When I got home, I'd made Tink and me pan-fried hamburgers for dinner, cleaned up and then went upstairs to change.

There was another spot in the city the fae frequented called, ironically, The Court on Canal. It was a little more laid back on the first level, featuring a bar that was surprisingly busy for fae on a Monday night. The second floor was not laid back. It was... well, I had seen some *things* up there. Things boric acid couldn't erase from my eyes or my brain.

The place was near the Quarter, a little hole in the wall that tourists and many of the locals overlooked. I'd spotted one of my targets there once before, but I'd lost sight of him once he left.

The Court on Canal couldn't be discovered on a Google search or on any must-see lists for when someone visited New Orleans.

The place was where nothing should be.

I'd found it on one of my mother's maps and one day I'd checked out the location and discovered that it was very much a real place—a place that not even the Order seemed to be aware of.

Once I was done finding the fae who'd attacked that night, I'd hand over the maps to Miles. I would tell him about The Court... and the other places. Just not yet.

I was hoping tonight would be as fruitful and not as eventful as Saturday night. I wasn't worried that I'd run into the Prince again, even though he so obviously knew it had been me Saturday night. I'd been to The Court numerous times and hadn't spotted him once.

Plus I was planning to keep an eye out for the missing younglings during my travels. I knew it was unlikely, at least I hoped, that I'd see one of them at The Court.

After a quick shower, I pinned my hair flat and got down to becoming someone else. Walking into the closet, I knew the perfect dress for tonight.

Black. Short. Simple.

Plucking it off the hanger, I wiggled into it, relieved to see that the material was some kind of stretchy knit as I tugged the hem down. It ended mid-thigh. I turned to the floor-length mirror and did the bend-over test.

Breasts pushed against the plummeting neckline, coming *this* close to falling out, and the cheeks of my butt peeked out under the stretchy material.

I straightened, smoothing my hands down the sides of the dress. Okay. Definitely not bending over in this in public.

Rolling my eyes, I grabbed my makeup case and went into the bathroom. The makeup took awhile, because I had to take my time to get it right, but when I was done, my face was virtually unrecognizable. Cheeks contoured until they were sharp and high. Lips outlined to be plumper and filled in with a color that was only a shade or two darker than my natural lips. I even filled in my eyebrows before tackling the eyes. I gave myself what I thought was a dark and smoky, mysterious look. Since I was leaving the contacts out, I put on some false eyelashes, and decided that if I didn't end up with a sty at some point during this, I was a mutant.

Back in the closet, I browsed the selection of wigs as I nibbled on my fingernail. Blonde. Red. Brown. Black. Purple. The vibrant wigs would draw too much attention at a place like The Court, so I picked the short, chin-length black wig and slipped it on, securing it in place and then combing it down so it was smooth and sleek.

The boots were... difficult. Made of some kind of stretchy material that covered the calves and knees with no zipper, I almost winged them across the bedroom trying to get them on. Sweat dotted my forehead by the time I was completely dressed.

And I was panting, a little out of breath as I slipped the iron cuff on my wrist.

Done, I turned to the mirror and grinned at my reflection. "I look like Aeon Flux," I said, cocking my head to the side. "A much sluttier version of Aeon Flux. Perfect."

* * * *

The Court on Canal looked like a, well, like a dump from the outside. The kind of place you'd expect to get a little food poisoning with your crawfish if you were brave enough to actually eat whatever they served, but the inside was all upscale.

Bar and booths made from wood refurbished from Katrina. Thick, leather-cushioned stools. Shiny, always clean high top round tables, and I'd never so much as seen a stray napkin in any of the private booths that sat back from the tables, lining the walls.

I carried only a black clutch as I strolled to the bar, wholly aware of the glances that lingered and followed while pretending that I wasn't.

It was weird to me. The knowledge that dressed like *this*, looking like *this*, I wasn't invisible. I was no longer a ghost, but I was....

What had the Prince said to me?

You are nothing but lies and façades.

Ugh.

He was right, and I really, seriously disliked him for that.

I wasn't this incarnation of myself. I could feel the warmth of embarrassment creeping up my throat in a prickly flush as I heard a low whistle from a man who was at one of the tables.

But I also wasn't the Brighton before the attack. She was gone, dying the night I should've died. Because while I was embarrassed by the attention, there was still a half grin that appeared on my lips.

Maybe the Prince was wrong.

Maybe I wasn't completely a façade.

I had no idea.

Climbing onto the stool as ladylike as humanly possible, I crossed one leg over the other and placed my clutch on the bar top.

A human bartender was behind the bar, but so was a fae. I wasn't quite sure if the female actually worked here, but she was the one I always saw when I came here, ferrying Nightshade back and forth to the non-human clientele.

Right now, she was carrying an entire tray of glasses to one of the booths along the wall. My gaze skipped away. There were a handful of fae among the humans chatting and drinking. None of them recognizable.

And definitely none of the younglings.

So far.

"What can I get you?"

I turned back to the bartender and smiled. He was young and his gaze was clear. Focused. Obviously not under any trance or control, but he had to know that not everyone who was served here was human. There was no way he couldn't, what with the Nightshade being served and what went on up on the second floor.

"A rum and Coke," I said.

"Coming right up." He picked up a glass and got to making the quick, easy drink. "Tab or pay now?"

"Cash." I opened my clutch and slid the money over to him. "Thank you."

The man smiled and then he was off, serving someone at the other end of the bar. Sipping my drink, I twisted around on the stool so I was facing the main bar floor, but was able to keep an eye on the back hallway, where the elevator serviced the second level. I pulled out my phone and pretended to be engrossed in it as I scanned the floor.

Within a few moments, two more fae entered the bar, their glamouring fading away to reveal their silvery, luminous skin. They made a beeline for the back hallway.

The second floor was a… different kind of service area, one that didn't just cater to fae looking for their dinner, but also sex.

Lots of sex.

Only once had I gone up to the second floor, and that had been pure luck, sneaking in behind a group of humans who were being led by two fae. Once was enough.

The humans I'd tagged along with had not been entranced. Based on their giggling and whispered dares to one another, they knew at least one of the things that went on upstairs.

"Excuse me."

Looking over my shoulder, I spied a man—a human man. He was older, maybe in his fifties? Tall with dark hair graying at the temples. Handsome, too, dressed in a very nice dark suit. A silver fox was what Ivy would've called him.

Pretty sure Tink would call him Daddy.

I immediately wanted to punch myself in the face after the image that conjured forth.

The man smiled, and wow he was handsome, and if I was anyone else, I would be extremely pleased with the attention. However, I wasn't here to meet silver foxes.

"I'm waiting for someone," I said apologetically.

Dipping his chin, he chuckled. "He said you might say something like that."

My brows lifted in surprise. "He?"

"I am not here to buy you a drink or to make an advance," he explained.

Oh.

Oh.

Well, this was awkward, and I sort of wanted to fling myself off the stool. "Sorry?"

He smiled tightly as his gaze drifted over my shoulder, to the bartender. He nodded. "My name is Everest. I am the owner of The Court and I'm here to escort you out."

Dumbfounded, all I could do was stare for a moment. "Excuse me?"

Everest moved closer, his brown eyes not nearly as warm as his smile. "You, my dear, are not welcome here."

A chill swept down my spine as I stared back at him. Only one possibility circled through my thoughts. Somehow, he knew I was a member of the Order and he facilitated what occurred here.

I played it cool, though, lifting my drink and taking a sip. "May I ask why?"

He didn't answer. Just smiled at me blandly. Out of the corner of my eyes, I saw a large man shift in our direction. Another human wearing another nice, expensive suit was moving our way. A bouncer.

And then it hit me. Everest had said…. My hand tightened on the damp glass as I leaned toward the owner. "He's here, isn't he?"

Everest continued to smile.

"The Prince," I said, and I said this loud enough to cause the woman at the table near us to turn and look.

The smile slipped from Everest's face and that was enough confirmation for me.

Son of a bitch.

I couldn't believe it. He'd been at Flux and now he was here? And not only was he here, but he was in a position to order the owner of this establishment to kick me out? An establishment, by the way, that was yet again frequented by the Winter fae?

At least I had a good reason to be here— a slightly psychotic reason but a reason, and the Prince was not going to get in my way.

Oh, hell to the no.

Anger flared to life like a solar storm. He was not going to interfere with me finding justice. No way in hell. "You can tell his royal Dickness that this is a public establishment and he does not get to dictate where I go and what I do."

The man's eyes widened slightly. "However, as the owner, I do get to dictate who stays here and who goes."

"True," I said, taking another long, healthy sip of my drink. I was raised to be a fine, upstanding Southern lady, but I was pissed. "Did he tell you what I am?"

Everest lifted a hand, stopping the bouncer from coming any closer.

"I don't know if he did, but I assure you that I can cause a lot of trouble for your *fine* establishment, and I mean a lot." I smiled now, all sugary sweet. "So unless you want that to happen, you can tell the Prince to go fuck himself."

Everest tilted his head slightly and a long heartbeat passed. Then he said, "You can tell him that yourself."

Chapter 12

The tiny hairs along the nape of my neck rose. I drew in a shallow breath as Everest stepped back, clasping his hands. Slowly, I lowered my drink and looked over my shoulder.

Standing not even a foot behind me was the Prince.

I couldn't help but notice immediately that he appeared different tonight. Hair pulled back from his face was a good look on him. A black silk shirt had replaced the thermal I'd seen him in, and that also was a good look.

But he was just about as angry as the last two times I'd seen him, so that hadn't changed.

Actually, he seemed angrier. "I can assure you, I have no attention of fucking myself tonight, *Sally*."

Steam practically shot from my ears at way he said my name—my fake name. "Good to know, but not my problem."

"Oh, but it is now your problem."

I drew back, eyes widening. "I have no idea how *that* is my problem."

Lifting blue eyes to Everest, he nodded. I didn't need to look to know the man had left.

Before I could say a word, he plucked the drink out of my hand and placed it on the bar. Then his hand wrapped around my empty one. I didn't dig my heels in like I wanted to, knowing that we already had several eyes on us.

My gaze dropped to where he held my hand as he guided me off the stool.

"You are becoming a pain in my ass," he said.

"I'm about to become a much bigger one. One you're going to need to see a doctor to treat. You try to make me leave," I said, lifting my gaze from his hand to his eyes, "I will make a scene in here so bad you'll spend the next year glamouring memories."

A muscle flexed along his jaw as his gaze searched my face. "You would, wouldn't you?"

"Yes. Now, if you'd unhand me, I think I might want another drink." In reality, my stakeout of The Court was ruined, but I would stay here half the night on principle alone. "And maybe some chicken wings." I had no idea if they served chicken wings here. "Then dessert. I'm definitely in the mood for dessert and none of those things include you."

The Prince threaded his fingers through mine, stopping me from yanking my arm free. "We need to have a chat."

"No, we don't."

"Oh, sunshine, we do."

Sunshine? My face puckered up. "There is nothing we need to talk about—" I gasped as he moved in so quick, so close, right there at the bar, in front of fae and human alike. Still holding my hand, he cupped my cheek with his other, splaying his fingers as he tilted my head back and lowered his.

Was he going… was he going to kiss me? That seemed like a bizarre response, but he lined his mouth right up with mine, and there were only inches between our lips. My heart rate shot into cardiac territory. "What are you doing?"

His warm breath danced over my lips as he spoke. "You should have left when you had a chance. Now, you and I are going to have a discussion that is way past due, and you're going to say yes and you're going to *behave*."

"Behave?" I sputtered.

He nodded as those thick lashes came down, shielding his eyes. "Don't test me."

My heart skipped a beat. "Is that a threat?"

"It's an advisory," he corrected.

"Same thing. Like totally the same thing."

His lips twitched as if he wanted to smile. "If you want a scene, I'll give you one. I'll throw you right over my shoulder, and with that dress?" Leaning back, I felt his gaze like a hot caress. "I don't think you'll want that."

I didn't.

I so didn't.

Seeming to sense that, he pulled me against the side of his body. The contact was jarring. Not because he did it roughly, because he didn't, but because feeling his body against mine stunned me.

Letting go of my hand, he then draped an arm over my shoulders like we were friends or even lovers as he steered me away from the bar. People were staring, human and fae alike, but the fae had more than just a reaction born of curiosity. As we walked near them, they backed away, giving us—giving the Prince—a wide berth. There was no mistaking the distrust and fear that pinched their striking features. They knew who the Prince was.

So, what was he doing here?

I held onto my clutch as we walked down the narrow hall, passing the restrooms and then the elevator. He walked me to a swinging door marked EMPLOYEES ONLY. With his free hand, he pushed open the door and we entered a small kitchen, staffed by cooks—human cooks. They only lifted their brows as he led me past them, narrowly dodging a waiter carrying a tray stacked with chicken wings.

So, they did have wings… and they looked yummy too.

My stomach grumbled, loud enough for the Prince to dip his head and look at me questioningly.

"Hungry?"

"No," I lied.

One side of his lips kicked up as we reached another door. That one opened to reveal another hallway and a narrow set of stairs.

"Should I be worried about where you're leading me?"

"You should always be worried." He dropped his arm. "Up the stairs."

"That's not reassuring," I told him, eyeing the dark staircase. "I'm getting stranger danger vibes right now."

"Is that all the vibes you're getting?" he asked.

I wrinkled my nose. "I don't know what you mean and I don't want to."

He smirked. "Up the stairs, Brighton."

The use of my real name startled me, even though we were alone. My gaze traveled from him to the staircase as I exhaled slowly. As crazy as it was, instinct told me that I was safe with the Prince. My instinct could be completely off base, but I also knew that if I made a run for it, I wasn't going to make it.

So I started up the stairs.

He said nothing as he walked behind me. We reached the next floor and entered a dark hallway where I could hear the steady thump of music coming from what sounded like the other side of the staircase. The hall also smelled like... fresh beignets. Part of me wanted to question that, but then the Prince brushed past me, the warmth of his body causing me to bite down on my lip. As he opened a door, I peeked around him. The room was circular, featuring a long, cushioned bench against the wall and a set dining table in the middle. There was a short rack glass on the table. Bright purple liquid filled half the glass. Nightshade.

"What kind of room is this?" I asked, folding my arms across my midsection.

"A private dining or party area. There are five of them on this floor. Nice hair, by the way." He stalked past me.

"Shut up," I muttered.

Smirking, he picked up his glass of Nightshade. "Still prefer the blond."

"I still don't care." I watched him walk to the wide cushioned bench against the wall and sit. "What are you doing here?"

"I could ask you the same thing, but I already know."

I ignored that. "This place is frequented by Winter fae and you're the Summer Prince. I don't understand how you can be here, hanging out and drinking with them."

He eyed me as he sipped from his drink. "I help Everest out here. Make sure none of the fae get out of hand."

Interesting. "And the Winter fae have no problem with you being here?"

"They usually don't see me until it's too late. Tonight is different because someone decided to refuse to leave."

"Perhaps you should've just left me be," I shot back as I started to pace. "So, what is this place, really? A front for fae to hang out and feed?"

"Everest is a... unique businessman who caters to all." He lowered the glass to his knee. "And he does so with the utmost discretion while providing a... safe place for both species."

"Safe place?"

"The fae can come here and see to their needs without harming humans in the process."

My lips parted. "I've seen what goes on up here."

He tilted his head. "And how, pray tell, did you find yourself on this floor? Didn't know the... activities up here were your kind of thing."

"They're not," I snapped, flushing. I turned from him, pacing away. "I got up here once, very carefully."

The Prince didn't respond to that immediately. "And when you got up that one time, did the humans look like they were here against their will?"

"Oh, so they're volunteers?" I faced him. "Want me to go grab you one of them?"

"I already had Everest do that for me."

My eyes narrowed on his faint smile.

"Sometimes, when Everest is expecting a certain... clientele, he will reach out to me to make sure there are additional resources here just in case."

I mulled that over. "How do the humans here keep this a secret if they aren't glamoured?"

"Who would believe them?"

"They could obtain evidence."

"They don't," he said, and then he took another drink. "You know, you won't be allowed back here now."

I smirked at that as I started pacing in front of him. "I'm not worried. I can get back in here if I want to."

"He'll be looking out for you."

"He won't recognize me."

"But I always will."

I shivered, unnerved by that. "Do you live here? Are you always here?"

The Prince didn't answer that.

"What do you think will happen if the Order ever discovers this place exists? They're not going to allow it to continue to operate."

"Who says those who need to know don't already?"

I stopped and stared at him. "Are you suggesting that Miles is aware of this place and hasn't shut it down?"

"I'm not suggesting anything. You filled in the blanks."

I snapped my mouth shut. My first reaction was not to believe him, but the Order had... It had lied about a lot of things and kept a lot of secrets. I knew that. So certain members knowing about this venue could be true.

"I knew it was you Saturday night, from the moment I saw you in that room."

"That much I figured," I said, but my stomach still dropped. "Why didn't you call me out, if you knew it was me?"

He was quiet for a moment. "I wanted to see how far you would let it go."

Heat blasted my cheeks. "Not very far."

The Prince lifted a brow. "My hand was right above your—"

"I know where your hand was," I snapped, cutting him off as that heat in my face hit my veins. "Trust me. It's something I won't forget."

"No doubt," he murmured, his lips curling into a faint smile.

My eyes narrowed. "As in not in a good way."

"I'm curious," he replied, watching me through hooded eyes. "If it wasn't in a good way, why did you allow it?"

I inhaled sharply. "I was pretending to be entranced."

"Hmm."

"I was!"

"If that's what you need to tell yourself."

I caught his meaning and I was this close to throwing my clutch at him. The dude was insufferable and mainly because he was so freaking right, and I sort of hated him for that. "I have no idea how you knew that was me."

"I... I just knew," he said like that was an acceptable answer.

Irritation flared to life and I decided right then and there I could also ask demanding, annoying questions as I dropped my clutch on the table. "So why were you at Flux? A club frequented by your enemy?"

He was dragging his thumb along the rim of his glass. "I was there looking for Tobias, but you already know that."

"Why were you looking for him?"

"Do you always ask so many questions?"

"You wanted to have this chat," I reminded him, crossing my arms again. "Why were you looking for him?"

"He knows how to find someone I need to speak with." His gaze dipped and there was a flash of straight, white teeth as he dragged them along his lower lip. I looked away as he said, "Alas, whatever information he had, he took that back to the Otherworld with him."

"Can't say I'm too torn about that."

"Of course not," he replied wryly.

"What information do you think he had?" I asked.

"He knows where a certain Ancient is that I would really love to murder."

My brows lifted at that. "Let me guess, an Ancient that sided with the Queen?"

The Prince nodded.

"Do you happen to know his name?"

A heartbeat passed. "Aric."

That name rang a bell. "Tobias did mention someone by the name of Aric."

Everything about The Prince became very still, so much so he could've stopped breathing. "Did he now?"

"Yes. Aric was coming to meet Tobias and the other fae. He would've been there within an hour."

"Are you serious?"

I nodded. "That was all they said about him."

The Prince cursed under his breath. "Perfect." Lifting the glass, he downed the rest of the Nightshade in one impressive swallow. "I know why you were at Flux and why you were here tonight. I know what Tobias did to you."

A ripple of shock rolled through me as I stared at him. "You don't know—"

"I know he was one of the five fae who attacked you and your mother." Leaning forward, he placed his empty glass on the table. He didn't settle back, and instead, placed his hands on his knees as he stared up at me. "I know that you're seeking revenge because of what they did. I know you're here tonight to see if you can find one of the other fae and I know you put yourself in ridiculously dangerous situations to get that revenge."

Arms falling to my sides, I took a step toward him and then stopped as my stomach twisted nauseously. "How do you...?" My throat thickened. "How do you know?"

He didn't answer for a long moment. "Because you are doing the same thing I am, but for different reasons."

I drew in a stuttering breath as a tremor rolled through my arms.

"I know what it's like to be consumed with revenge and the need to seek justice against those who have done you wrong so terribly. I understand that. It is why I am searching for Aric. He was once a trusted friend of mine, and I know he is the one who set me up to fall to the Queen's spell," he explained, and I felt pressure clamp down on my chest. "I know he's still alive and he's here. I will find him and I will kill him for what he has done to me. And if I ever get my hands on the Queen, I will rip her limb from limb."

That might sound shocking, but I couldn't fault him for wanting that. Not with what she had done to him—made him do.

"Well," I said hoarsely, hating the feel of the bitter knot creeping into my throat, "I guess we have that in common."

"I know what it is like to lie awake all night, consumed with what you could've done to change what happened and how you could've stopped it."

"How could you have stopped it though?" I asked, my question genuine. "You were injured in a battle, right? Weakened?"

"Not only do I believe he is spending every moment trying to aid the Queen's return, it was Aric who shoved a sword right through my chest."

My eyes widened. Swords? Man, the Otherworld always sounded archaic but swords? I shook my head. "The Queen placed you under an enchantment. You didn't have a choice."

"I know everything I did while under her spell. Every person I hurt or killed. Every horrific act I committed." Thick lashes lowered, shielding his gaze as my heart turned over in my chest. "I remember in vivid detail what I put Ivy through."

Pressing my lips together, I blinked back unexpected wetness. I couldn't imagine what he was going through. In a way, I knew it was worse than what happened to me and my mother. He'd been the bad guy. He'd done terrible things and now he lived with the guilt even though it hadn't been his fault.

So I told him that. "It wasn't your fault."

"Tell me," he said. "When you look at me, tell me you don't think about how I kidnapped Ivy? Tell me you don't think about all those Order members I killed with my own hands. Tell me—"

"I do," I admitted, flinching. "I do think of those things, but I also realize it wasn't your fault. You had no control. You didn't have a choice," I repeated, meaning it.

"And you were outnumbered by creatures a hundred times stronger and faster than you," he said, meeting my gaze. "What could you have done differently?"

"If I had been better trained, I could've fought back," I said without a second of hesitation.

He stared at me for a long moment. "Even better trained, you most likely would've died, sunshine. You have a soul of a warrior, but that is not enough."

A soul of a warrior?

That was... that was kind of a nice thing to say.

"You need to stop this, Brighton."

Biting down on the inside of my lip, I looked away as I shook my head. "Are you going to stop looking for Aric? Are you going to move and take the higher road and not seek revenge?"

"I'm different."

I rolled my eyes. "Why? Because you're the Prince?"

The faint smile didn't reach his eyes. "Yes."

Irritated that he understood why I needed to do what I had to, but was trying to stop me, I threw up my hands. "You can't stop me."

He arched a brow at that as he sat back. "I can stop you."

Caring and sharing time was so over. "You know what? I don't even get why you care. We barely know each other. You're the Prince, and I'm just... I'm just me. I'm a—" I almost blurted out ghost, but stopped myself.

"You're what?" Curiosity crept into his features.

I shook my head. "It doesn't matter. I appreciate your concern. I do. It's unexpected, but I appreciate it. It's not going to change—"

"You're what?" he repeated.

Pressing my lips together, I shook my head in frustration.

"What were you about to say?" he persisted.

"I'm just a ghost," I blurted out, surprised that I allowed the words to take flight, because once spoken, you couldn't take it back. "That's who I was before the attack and..."

He was watching me intently. "And you're not a ghost anymore?"

"I don't know what I am anymore," I admitted, blinking back the stupid burn of tears again. "And I don't even know why I'm telling you this. I don't even like you."

"You don't even know me."

"You know? You're right. And no matter what you say, you don't know me either." I started for the door. "I'm done with this conversation. I'm done with your interference. You do whatever you want to do and I'll do whatever I need to do. Goodbye, Prince."

"You're right." A muscle flexed a long his jaw. "You're just a human," he said, and the way he said that made the word human sound like a venereal disease. "In your own words, you're already half dead. I won't stop you from finishing that job."

Chapter 13

The Prince's parting words stung more than they should have as I stared at him. There was a part of me, a stupid, tiny part of me that was hurt by those words. The rational part of me knew that was stupid because I'd called myself a ghost.

But to hear him say it?

Brighton from two years ago would've never found herself in this situation in the first place, but if she did, she would've definitely run from the room to lick her wounds no matter how stupid those wounds were.

But I wasn't her.

And I might not know what the hell I was anymore, but in that moment, I wasn't a ghost. Not anymore.

I met his gaze and then smiled as I slowly lifted my hand and flipped him off.

His nostrils flared.

With that, I pivoted around and stalked out of the weird room with my head high. The moment I yanked open the stupid door, my mind immediately went berserko on me, replaying every word we exchanged.

My head was a freaking mess as I slammed the door shut behind me, mainly because I'd never shared with anyone else what I shared with him. I had no explanation for why, none that made sense at least. I couldn't even believe that I'd spoken those words to him. Embarrassment rose as I stalked down the dark hallway, toward where I remembered the stairway was, hearing the thump of music once again. As I opened the door, I briefly fantasized about racing back into that room and spin kicking him in the face.

That fantasy was probably why I didn't realize the stairwell wasn't empty until it was too late.

A shadow peeled off the wall and came at me fast and hard. I didn't even get the chance to engage the cuff and release the stake. My right arm was twisted behind my back as an icy hand curled around my neck.

A burst of panic punched through my chest as I was flipped around and my front pushed against the wall. The side of my face slammed into the cool brick. Stinging pain exploded from my nose and I tasted blood in the back of my throat.

"I recognized you," the voice said, and I couldn't place it. "You were in the club Saturday night. You went into the room with Tobias. Your hair was red then. Different eye color, too."

Hell.

Shock that my disguise had been seen through gave way to finely honed instinct. Going limp, my sudden weight caught the fae off guard. He stumbled back a step, giving me the room I needed. Bringing my legs up, I planted them in the wall and used it as a springboard. The fae slammed into the wall behind him, the impact jarring his hold loose enough for me to break it.

I fell forward, my knees cracking off the cement. Knowing I only had seconds, I shifted my weight to my palms as I looked over my shoulder, kicking my leg out. My booted heel connected with the fae's midsection, sending him back again to the wall with a grunt.

Popping to my feet, I engaged the cuff bracelet as I whirled around.

The door to the hallway suddenly swung open, blocking my view of the fae and then the door wasn't blocking my view.

It was the Prince.

He seemed to know what was happening, because he went straight for the fae. He was so fast that literally only seconds had passed between him stepping into the cramped stairwell and placing his hands on either side of the fae's neck, snapping it.

The fae slumped to the floor, twitching, and then tumbled down the narrow flight of steps, coming to stop in a twitchy heap on the landing.

My mouth was hanging open as the Prince casually pulled his phone out of his pocket, hit a few buttons and then said, "Everest, I have some trash that needs to be taken out. Back staircase."

Then, slowly, he turned toward me. "You're bleeding."

I touched my nose. It was sore, but nothing major. "I'm fine."

"You've had worse."

I had and I didn't need to confirm that. "How did you know what was happening?"

A moment passed. "Luck."

My eyes narrowed, and for some reason, I didn't believe him. He knew something was happening in this stairwell; how was left to be determined.

His head cocked to the side. "Why did he attack you?"

Glancing down at the spasming fae, I winced. "He recognized me from Flux. I don't know how, but I think he might've been with Tobias."

"I killed all those fae."

"He may have left before you got there." I lifted a shoulder. "You know I can take care of him."

"Everest will handle it."

I thought that was unnecessary, but whatever. I disengaged the iron cuff as I dragged my gaze from the fae, more annoyed than anything else. I hated to admit it to myself, but if that fae had seen through my disguises, there was a good chance that another fae could.

Wiping the blood off my nose with the back of my hand, I then bent and picked up my dropped clutch.

"A soul of a warrior," he murmured, repeating what he'd said earlier.

I didn't know how to respond to that as I looked at him, discovering that he was staring at me intently once more.

"But like I said before, it's not enough."

That I knew how to respond to. "I was doing just fine before you showed up, just so you know."

A tight smile formed, one I imagined a parent gave a child when they came in dead last during a race. "You hungry?"

I blinked. "What?"

"Are you hungry?" he repeated, angling his large body toward mine. "For food." Amusement was clear in his tone.

"I didn't need the second part clarified. Thanks," I muttered.

"I know this place down the street that has the most amazing crab cakes. Would you like to join me?" he asked, and in the dim light of the stairwell, those pale eyes were piercing.

I should say no.

I definitely should say no for a multitude reasons.

"Okay," I said instead, because I was an idiot and honestly, the offer knocked me off guard. "I guess."

One side of his lips kicked up. "Good, but I just have one request."

"You invited me to grab something to eat, but you have one request?"

"I do," he said. "I want you."

My eyes widened as the heat from earlier returned in full force, and goodness, that was annoying... and a little frightening. "Excuse me?"

"I want you to be yourself. I don't want *this*." He gestured in the general direction of my head. "I want you to be... *you*."

* * * *

I'd used a restroom on the second floor to change... back into myself. Of course, I wasn't able to get rid of the makeup. That required near industrial strength makeup remover, but I took off the wig and unpinned my hair, shaking it out. That was the best I could do, and I wasn't even sure why I'd done it.

Maybe it was because no one... no one ever seemed interested in me before, the real me, that the request stunned me into complying. That was the best reasoning I could come up with as I found myself sitting across from the Prince in a brightly lit Creole House, toying with the paper wrapper from my straw as the amazing scent of spicy seafood had my stomach rumbling.

We were... we were getting a lot of looks. Strange ones. Long ones with raised eyebrows. I figured it was partly because the Prince was so big and so freaking nice to look at, that people were probably wondering if he was a celebrity they couldn't place. I also figured that some of the looks were due to the fact I looked like a hooker.

I like to think I at least looked like an expensive hooker.

"You're nervous," the Prince commented after we placed an order for crab cakes and, per the Prince's request, a crawfish platter.

I glanced up at him. Was I nervous? Uh, yes. I was currently sitting across from the Prince in a restaurant looking halfway like my normal self, and I really had no idea how I'd ended up here. "Do you smell it?"

A faint smile appeared. "Don't need to. You're building a compost pile over there."

Frowning, I glanced down and saw that I did have a significant pile of torn paper in front of me. I dropped my hands to my lap and drew in a shallow breath as I lifted my gaze. "I don't... I don't think this is a good idea."

His stare was unwavering. "It's probably not."

My heart skipped at the agreement. I don't know what I was expecting him to say, but I wasn't thinking he was going to agree. "You asked me to join you."

"I did."

I stared at him. "So why did you ask me to join you if you think it's a bad idea?"

He leaned against the booth, tossing his arm along the back. "Because good ideas are ideas rarely wanted... or needed."

Flattening my hands on my thighs, I wasn't sure how to respond that. "Okay."

"Why did you agree if you think it's a bad idea?"

I let out a dry laugh. "Honestly? I don't know."

The faint smile reappeared. "So, since you were recognized by the fae tonight, will that be enough for you to rethink what you're doing?"

"Is that why you asked me to come here?" I picked up my diet Coke and took a sip. "To involve yourself yet again in something that does not concern you?"

"It concerns me."

I put my glass down. "How is that?"

He dipped his chin and stared at me through lowered lashes. "That's not going to deter you, is it? The added risk."

Shaking my head, I lifted a shoulder. "Do you want me to tell you what you want to hear or the truth?"

There was a flicker of amusement that crossed his face. "You risk too much."

"I haven't risked nearly enough."

"How do you see that?"

I leaned forward, placing my hands on the table. "I've spent thirty years playing it safe."

His brows lifted. "That's your logical reasoning for putting your life on the line?"

Sounded pretty illogical, but whatever. "You know why I must do this, risk or not. Just like you would go after Aric or the Queen even if it meant your death."

A muscle ticked along his jaw. "As I said before, it's different." There was a pause. "I remember," he said. "I remember the first time I saw you."

A shiver danced across my shoulders as I lifted my gaze to his.

"You were scared of us—of me and my brother, but mostly me. You stood in the corner of Tanner's office, not daring to come close," he continued, and that was true. Both had scared me, but especially him. "And then I saw you the night we fought the Queen. You were still afraid, but you helped my brother. You helped my brother and me even knowing what I'd done while under the Queen's control."

The night resurfaced. Prince Fabian had been severely injured by the Queen and he'd needed to get back to Hotel Good Fae. I had offered to help. "I didn't do much. I just drove you guys back to the hotel."

He leaned forward, his gaze never leaving mine. "You were afraid of us. You were unsure of us, but you still helped us when it was needed. That is doing everything and that is why I owe you an apology."

"You do?"

"For what I said about you looking for the younglings and knowing how important it was," he explained. "I shouldn't have doubted you, not when I know you will come through when needed."

While his doubt had been frustrating, it was understandable. "It... not a big deal."

"It is." The Prince sat back. "In my experience, it is."

I didn't know what to say, so I said nothing as I stared at my glass of soda, watching the little bubbles race to the surface.

"It would be such a shame for the world to lose someone... someone like you, especially after being given a second chance."

Air hitched in my throat. That was yet another word of kindness from him that I didn't know how to process. "That's nice of you to say, but you... you don't know me well enough to think that."

"I am hardly ever wrong about these kinds of things."

A laugh escaped me. "Okay. Even if that is the case, like I said before, I don't understand why you care this much to have this conversation again. Remember? I'm just a human woman and I'm already half dead."

His jaw worked as those lashes lowered again. "I should not have spoken those words."

"Why? Because they were ignorant?"

"Because what you said about yourself is a lie."

I stilled. "What do you mean?"

A long moment passed, so much so that I thought he wouldn't answer, but then those thick lashes lifted and those eyes seemed to see straight through me once more. "You're not a ghost. You never could be one, not when you burn as brilliant as the sun."

Chapter 14

It was Friday evening—pizza night in the Jussier household, a tradition carried on for many years and now continued with Tink and me. After eating, I'd gone upstairs and changed into warmer clothes because I planned on heading out tonight to see if I could do some recon on the other two fae I was still looking for and the missing younglings.

I'd checked in with Faye on Wednesday and there'd been no word from any of the missing fae. And with each passing day, I could tell she was losing hope and becoming more convinced that the Order had harmed them, rather intentionally or unintentionally.

Even the Prince hadn't said as much, but I knew he probably speculated the same.

Then again, the Prince was adept at giving vague answers.

Over the last couple of days, I did everything in my power not to think about what we'd said to each other. What we'd admitted. Or the dinner that had started out awkward and ended rather normally, with me somehow talking about all the TV shows Tink was addicted to. And I definitely wasn't thinking about how he said I could never be a ghost.

That I was as brilliant as the sun.

Nope. Wasn't thinking about that or how no one, utterly no one had ever said something like that to me. I also wasn't lying awake at night thinking about how he... he wanted to spend time with *me*. The real me. I wasn't thinking about that at all. Nope.

I hadn't seen the Prince since our dinner of very yummy crab cakes and crawfish. Half of me had expected to run into him when I was out Wednesday night, but he hadn't magically appeared out of thin air like he had before. And that was a good thing.

Wasn't like I was actually looking forward to seeing him.

So I decided to focus on the important stuff, like what I learned about this Ancient named Aric who might or might not be trying to make contact with the Queen.

And that was really bad news.

The problem was if I talked to Miles, he'd question how I came about the information. That put what I was trying to accomplish in jeopardy. If I had to confide in someone who just might understand where I was coming from it would be Ivy and she would be back in the city in about a week.

I had time.

Anyway, I'd only been gone twenty minutes tops, so I was rather shocked by the current condition of the kitchen when I returned.

Crossing my arms and then unfolding them before crossing them again, I looked around the room. I took a breath and then exhaled slowly. "Why does it look like the FBI raided my kitchen while I was upstairs?"

And that's what it seriously looked like.

All the cabinet doors were open. Glasses were pushed around. Plates askew. Tupperware on the verge of toppling onto the counters. Pots and pans in the lower cabinets turned so their handles were jutting out.

"Well, you see, it's kind of a long story." Tink sat on the edge of the island, his legs swinging and his wings twitching while the scent of fried meat mingled with the peach-scented candle that was burning behind him. Dixon was lying beside him, his long tail swishing idly.

I turned to him and opened my mouth, but I was at a loss.

"Dixon and I were playing hide and go seek."

That explanation didn't help either. "How do you play hide and go seek with a cat?"

Dixon's ears flattened as Tink gasped dramatically. "Are you suggesting that Dixon doesn't have the brain capacity to play hide and go seek?"

"Dixon is a cat—a very smart cat, but a cat." I shook my head as I walked over to the small kitchen table. "You are so cleaning this up."

"I was planning to." Tink took flight, following me over to the table. He landed on the back of the white chair. "What are you doing? And don't lie and say you have a date."

"I'm actually going to walk the Quarter," I said, deciding not to lie.

"There's some younglings that have gone missing and I'm going to see if I can find any of them."

His brows knitted together. "Fabian mentioned something about that, but he didn't seem too concerned."

"Well, Tanner and Faye are. They contacted the Order."

"Oh, and I bet the Order cares sooo much about a few missing Summer fae." He walked along the narrow back of the chair like it was a balance beam. "They were basically 'not my problem'?"

"Pretty much. That's why I was going to head out. The chance that I see any of them is pretty nil, but it can't hurt to try." Glancing back to the island after I heard the soft thump of Dixon dropping to the floor, I made another quick decision. "Do you want to come with me?"

Tink halted, one little leg up in the air. His forehead wrinkled as he looked up at me and then glanced down to where Dixon was weaving himself around my ankles. "Nah, I need to clean up the kitchen."

"You sure?"

He nodded as he flew up so he was eye level with me. His wings moved quietly through the air. "Yeah, and I discovered this new show that I'm only a few episodes into."

Tink gave me a lot of crap about going out hunting without him, but Tink didn't go out often. Sometimes I wondered if he had some kind of phobia surrounding the outside human world and that was why he didn't travel to Florida with Fabian. Then again, he had traveled with Ivy and team to San Diego when they were searching down leads to stop the Queen.

"What show?" I asked.

"Santa Clarita Diet. It's about this woman who becomes a zombie, but she's not like a Walking Dead zombie. She's basically trying to live her best life with her husband and daughter as a flesh-eating zombie."

"Okay." I drew the word out. "Sounds like you have a fun evening planned."

"I do." Tink flew with me as I went into the small mudroom that exited onto the porch and picked up my Saints cap. "Will you keep in contact with me?"

Grinning, I pulled the cap on and shoved my ponytail up under it. "Of course." Watching Tink when he was this size use a cellphone was quite amusing. "I won't be out too late."

"Coolio," he murmured, zooming back into the kitchen. A second later, I heard him yell, "Giddy-up Dixon, we must conquer the kitchen and then it's Netflix time!"

Shaking my head, I picked up my keys and shoved them into the back pocket of my jeans. I pulled my peacoat from a hook and shoved my arms through it. The last thing I put on was the iron cuff. That was a just-in-case thing. I started for the door and then stopped, pulling out a gray basket. I snatched up an iron stake and placed it into the pocket of my jacket. That was another just in case.

I slipped out the side door and, after making sure it was locked behind me, I turned around and halted.

An odd feeling crept along the nape of my neck as I stared at the narrow pathway that connected the front yard to the courtyard out back. Tiny bumps rose all along my body as I shivered, not from the cold but from… from the feeling of being watched.

I walked to the end of the porch and saw no one in the courtyard or anywhere near the house. My gaze flicked to the house next door. All the curtains were in place. Coming back to the side door, I checked yet again that it was locked and then made my way to the front of the house.

As I stepped off the porch and walked toward the front yard, I told myself it was just my imagination, but I couldn't shake the eerie sensation.

Couldn't shake it at all.

* * * *

Emerald green beads whizzed through the air as the drunken college-aged guy in a one-piece hot pink bathing suit twirled in the middle of Bourbon Street, his white sneakers pounding off the pavement. The suit was cut high along the hips and the front was nothing more than two panels of cloth held together by a jeweled clasp. It was not the kind of bathing suit made to wear when someone actually planned on swimming.

Or made to wear on a chilly March evening.

The man spun, winging another strand of beads into the night as the crowd cheered him on. The back of the suit showed more of the man's ass than it covered, but I had to say, it was a nice ass.

Mardi Gras had ended over a month ago, so I really had no idea what this dude was doing with the beads and the bathing suit. But it was Friday night in the French Quarter, so I knew I was going to see far weirder crap before the night was over.

Leaning against the brick wall of The Swamp, I sipped my ginger ale as someone shrieked happily from the courtyard behind me. Raucous laughter followed, and I figured someone had gotten thrown from the mechanical bull.

One of these days I imagined that bull was going to snap and pitch a person head first through a window.

Grinning at that because I was a terrible person, I took another sip of the carbonated goodness as I scanned the packed streets, looking for people that weren't quite... people. I reached into the pocket of my lightly lined cotton peacoat, feeling a sharp trill curl down my spine as my fingers brushed over the warm, slim piece of metal.

There was an eight-inch iron stake in my pocket and I was so not afraid to use it.

I couldn't help but wonder what I would be thinking if I had been out here two years ago. I wanted to be doing this, but I didn't have the lady balls. Not only would the Order members have laughed like deranged hyenas, I would've laughed... and had a minor panic attack simultaneously, because I'm a good multitasker like that.

Now I was more than capable of patrolling for the Order, but they didn't know that and if they did, it wouldn't matter. Just look at how they'd treated me today. Even if they saw me in action, it wouldn't change their views.

In their eyes, I wasn't the same as them and I'd never be ready to take to the streets. Not at my age. It was so ridiculous, considering the Order had been nearly decimated.

I drew in a shaky breath and it got hung up on the knot that had formed in my throat as my gaze swiveled back to the mayhem in the middle of the street.

The guy in the hot pink bathing suit had no idea how close the world had come to chaos. None of the people partying in the streets, laughing, drinking, and shouting knew that so many people—people I missed with every breath I took—had their lives brutally ended in an unknown war with the fae.

Hell, they didn't even know that the fae were a real and almost always deadly thing that walked among them, blending in and hunting them. I never once wondered what it would be like to not know there were things out there that could end your life in a snap of their fingers, but I guess there was a blissfulness in that ignorance.

Across the street, a woman stepped out from the throng of people milling up and down the narrow sidewalk, dressed in black leather pants and a tight black thermal.

Crap.

Recognizing Jackie, I slinked back against the wall and reached up, tugging the bill of my Saints' ball cap lower. The dark-skinned Order member stood on the curb, arms crossed as she watched Hot Pink Bathing Suit Guy, out of beads now, bend over and twerk.

Jackie was grinning now, but if she saw me, she wouldn't be smiling anymore. She'd legit kick my butt and then drag said butt back home, because she'd know what I was doing out here.

Which was utter bullshit. Logic dictated that the Order needed all the help they could get.

But I wasn't out here to patrol. I really was keeping an eye out for the younglings. I'd saved their photos to my phone, and pretty much had their faces committed to memory at this point. I figured if they were anywhere down here getting into trouble, they would be near Bourbon or Royal.

Part of me didn't think it would be a big deal if Jackie saw me or not. Probably would never cross her mind that I'd be out patrolling or anything like that. She'd probably think I was out grabbing dinner or something.

I couldn't risk it though.

Because if she did figure out what I was doing, I risked her discovering my other extracurricular activities.

Pushing away from the wall, I shoved both hands into my pockets as I pivoted to the left and headed for St. Louis Street. Crossing the street, I kept an eye out as I made my way toward Royal. It was so easy spotting tourists in the winter months. Locals were bundled up even though it was in the low fifties. Visitors were in T-shirts and jeans and skirts, obviously hailing from much colder climates. The Summer fae were the same, all toasty in their heavy jackets and wool beanies. You'd think it was below freezing seeing them, but the Winter fae? This wasn't nearly cold enough for them.

And it didn't take me long to find one.

Nearing Royal, I spotted the first suspicious fae of the evening and it wasn't the fact the young man was wearing a thin shirt and worn jeans that gave him away as a not-so-friendly fae. At least this fae was a normal one.

A shudder worked its way through me as I picked up my pace. I knew that the fae in front of me was not of the Summer Court, and it had nothing to do with how he dressed. It was the fact he was stalking a young woman who appeared to have just gotten off work from one of the many restaurants, her all-black server clothing partially obscured by one of those fluffy down jackets.

I wasn't technically patrolling, but if I saw a fae going after someone, I wasn't just going to stand back and do nothing.

I was so not about that kind of life anymore.

My fingers curled around the thickest part of the stake as the distance between us evaporated. Fae hated all things iron. Just a mere touch would sting them, continuous contact would burn them.

And this fae was about to meet the business end of the stake. A direct hit to the chest wouldn't kill them, but it would send them back to the Otherworld. And with the doorways to the Otherworld currently sealed, that was as good as dead.

Well, until the Queen decided to make another run for taking over the world and blew the doors wide open, but totes as good as dead until—

The young male glanced over his shoulder, not paying a lick of attention to me, but I stumbled.

Holy crap, I recognized the fae.

It was Elliot—the missing cousin's friend. I was sure it was totally him, but that didn't make sense. He was of the Summer Court and lived at Hotel Good Fae. And he and his parents didn't feed or prey upon humans.

That didn't mean they couldn't. It was a choice they made, so that meant it was a choice they could change at any time. And who knew how many times that had happened in the past? It wasn't exactly something anyone in the Order tracked.

Elliot suddenly hung a sharp left, slipping between two buildings, into a narrow alley. The girl was almost upon the intersection of Royal now, no longer of interest to him. Maybe I was wrong about the whole stalking thing. That was good news, but what the hell was he doing and where had he been?

Irritation spiked. Everyone worried the Order had killed this boy or that some other horrific thing had happened to him, but here he was, partying it up in the Quarter? So freaking annoying.

I hesitated for a moment at the mouth of the alley, knowing that following a fae, even if they were friendly, into an alley wasn't exactly the brightest thing to do.

Jackie would follow him.

Ivy sure as hell would do it.

I could do it.

I *needed* to do it.

Squaring my shoulders, I drew in a shallow breath and followed him into the dimly lit passageway, prepared to let loose a lecture my mother would've been proud of—

Wait.

My steps slowed as a frown pulled at my mouth. The alley was a dead end, blocked by another brick building. Where in the hell did he go? I walked farther, past a large dumpster. Unless he was hiding in here, he'd....

Slowly, I lifted my gaze to the two- and three-story buildings crowding the alley that smelled like stale beer and poor life choices. A fae could easily climb or jump that height, but not a fae who wasn't feeding. A fae who didn't feed was stronger than a human, yes, but they didn't have super jumping—

Thump.

Tiny hairs along the nape of my neck rose as I heard something land softly behind me. Instinct roared to life as I clutched the iron stake and spun around.

Elliot stood in the center of the alley, in the spot that had been empty seconds ago. Startled, I took a step back. For him to have made that jump...

"You're following me," he stated.

Apparently I had not been as stealthy as I thought. "Well, yes—"

"I know you," he interrupted, arms loose at his sides as he drifted closer.

He did? I didn't recall meeting him, but there was a chance he'd seen me at Hotel Good Fae in the days and weeks leading up to the battle with the Queen. But that was two years ago.

"I'm not sure if we've met." My heart started hammering in my chest. "But I know your parents."

His head cocked to the side, and in the darkness, his eyes looked like black pits.

The hair along the back of my neck was still standing. "Your parents are worried about you, Elliot. Where have you been?"

"My parents?" He straightened his head and moved even closer. "Those stupid posers? Those weak wannabe humans? They're not my parents. Not anymore."

Uh oh.

"And I know you. You're with the Order." Elliot hissed like a cornered cat, a very large and very pissed-off cat, and even in the shadowy alley, I could see the sabertooth-like teeth descending from his gaping mouth.

Oh crap, Elliot was so not on Team Good Fae anymore. Not at all.

There was no chance to question why in the hell Elliot was suddenly all psychotic. Yanking at the stake, I realized too late I should've just engaged the cuff. Elliot launched into the air like a rocket. In one stuttered heartbeat, he was on me, his body crashing into mine. The impact knocked me off my feet and my baseball cap off my head, and I went down hard. Air punched out of my lungs.

Never let them get you on the ground.

Those words from the most basic of trainings roared through my head as my eyes opened wide.

I'd been on my back before. I knew how this ended.

Elliot crouched over me, gripping the collar of my jacket. Our gazes connected—

Something... something was wrong with his eyes. They weren't the pale blue of the fae. They *were* pitch black, so dark I couldn't even see the irises.

I'd never seen anything like that, not in person or in the many books I'd studied on the fae.

Panic sparked deep in my chest as I struggled to get my stupid hand out of my pocket. The wicked sharp edge caught on the interior of my coat, snagging and tearing the cloth. He lifted me upward as he swung a fist back. Elliot punched down, but I flung myself up and over. His fist slammed into the pavement as my forehead cracked off his.

He cursed as he jerked.

Rocking backward, I ignored the bitter taste of fear and swung my legs up, wrapping them around his narrow waist. Using my weight, I flipped Elliot off me as I rolled. On top of him, I reared back as I pulled the stake out, tearing the pocket in the process. I lifted it high, preparing to jam it straight through his chest.

Elliot's fist connected with my stomach. The burst of pain stole my breath, but I powered through it, swinging the dagger downward.

The fae was fast, slamming his hands into my chest. I flew backward, landing on my butt. Before I could recover, Elliot shot off the ground and was on me once more. I'd held onto the dagger, gritting my teeth as his hand came down on my throat, his fingers digging into my windpipe. I swung the stake around, thinking a head shot would do the trick.

His hand suddenly left my throat and then Elliot was flipping through the air as if invisible hands had snatched him up.

Gasping for breath, I rolled onto my side, my free hand splaying across the pavement. Several strands of blonde hair had slipped free from my ponytail, blocking one eye.

Elliot was rising to his feet. He spun and then his body jerked back a step. He was frozen for a moment and then his body just caved into itself, sucking itself back into the Otherworld with a faint pop and sizzle.

"Holy smokes…." Breathing heavy, I started to sit up. Gratefulness warred with dread. Obviously an Order member had intervened, which was great, but also meant I was busted, so freaking busted.

A tall, broad shadow strolled forward. The light of the lamp sliced over an iron dagger and black gloves. Gloves? It was cold, but not *that* cold.

Wait.

I started to rise as I lifted my gaze. Every muscle in my body locked up. I saw who'd come to my quite unnecessary rescue and anxiety exploded like a buckshot along with a hefty amount of WTF.

Now I understood the gloves.

It wasn't an Order member who'd intervened.

He now stood under the lamp, and I would swear the light intensified as it shone down on him, as if powered by his presence.

The Prince stood before me. "We meet yet again."

Chapter 15

My hand tightened on the iron stake as the buzz of anticipation swept through me. No way should I be excited to see him—and the mere thought of that was so utterly confusing—but I was.

So I ignored the feeling. "You totally just stabbed Elliot."

His brows lowered as he hooked the stake to what I assumed was some hidden sheath. "I did."

"You do realize he was one of the missing younglings, right?"

"You do realize you were trying to stab him in the head, which would have roughly the same result as what I did?"

Okay. He had a good point.

"And you do realize he was about to choke the life out of you?"

"I completely had that handled," I said. "Completely."

"Is that so?" He folded his arms across his chest as he stared down his nose at me. "You looked like you had everything under control with his hands around your throat. Just like you looked like you had everything under control Monday night, when—"

"I had that fae under control and I *was* about to stab him in the head," I reminded him. "Before I was rudely interrupted."

The Prince cocked his head to the side. "Saving your life is rudely interrupting you?"

"I didn't need my life saved, thank you very much." Pushing to my feet, I met his stare with a glare I was rather proud of.

"That's not the thank you I was expecting, but I'll take it." His lips curled into a smirk as my mouth clamped shut. "What were you doing out here, Brighton? I thought we had an understanding."

"We did? Because I'm pretty sure that I never gave you any

indication that we had an understanding." I turned away from him and then gasped, stumbling a step back. He was in front of me. "Jesus."

"Not quite." His arms were at his sides.

"Ha. Ha." I rolled my eyes as I fought a grin.

"Why are you out here, Brighton?" He was not nearly as amused as I was. "You're not an Order member."

"I am an Order member." And whatever amusement I was feeling evaporated. My hand around the stake twitched and I resisted the urge to lob it at his smirking face—his very attractive, smirking face. "I was born into the Order and I am willing to give my life to fulfill my duty to the Order."

"I stand corrected," he demurred, dipping his chin. "However, you are not a hunter."

"Gee, thanks, Captain Obvious."

He stared down at me.

Exhaling roughly, I shook my head as anger and a good dose of embarrassment churned inside me. I was a real Order member. God. "Look, thanks for getting involved when you weren't needed, but I've got things to do that don't involve standing in an alley talking to you."

"Really? What are those things you have to do? Go to Flux? The Court? Risk being seen again?"

I ran my tongue along the roof of my mouth. "Actually, no. And you know what, why are you out here? How did you just happen to be in this alley? Not exactly a place on the must-see list of New Orleans. I'm beginning to think—" I sucked in an unsteady breath. I hadn't heard him move, but he'd shifted closer.

"Think what?" he asked.

I tossed the stake up and then caught it. "It's just weird."

"What?"

"How in the last week, you've nearly showed up everywhere I've been. It's almost like you're following me."

"What if I was?"

I almost dropped the stake as my gaze flew to his face. His expression was unreadable and I couldn't tell if he was being serious or not. "Really? That's not creepy or anything."

His sigh was so heavy I was surprised it didn't shake the buildings. "You shouldn't be out here."

"What do you want from me?" I challenged. "I mean, really? Are we going to have this conversation every five minutes?"

"What do I want from you?" An emotion flickered across his face, parting his lips. "That's a loaded question."

I started to frown as I tossed the stake up again. "Not really."

His hand shot out with a speed that was both unnerving and impressive, snatching the stake out of the air with gloved fingers.

"Hey!" I reached for it.

The Prince deftly avoided my grasp. "That is incredibly distracting—"

"It's not my fault you can't multitask," I muttered.

"And incredibly dangerous," he continued. "I really don't want to see it go through your hand."

I popped my hands onto my hips. "It wasn't going to go through my hand."

"Rather be safe than sorry." He smiled tightly at me, and that just annoyed me to no end.

I started to ask for my stake back, but he spoke again. "You're not a hunter," he repeated, changing the subject. "Why were you out here?"

Back to that again. I sighed. "I wasn't out here patrolling. I was seeing if I could find one of the missing younglings, which I did. However, that didn't end well."

"No, it did not."

Knocking a strand of hair back from my face, I glanced at the mouth of the alley. "I thought it was a Winter fae first because he was following a woman, so I kept an eye on him—and yes, I know, I'm not a hunter, but I'm not going to walk away and leave someone to fend for themselves."

"You should have."

My head swung back to his. "I didn't ask for your opinion."

His eyebrow rose.

"Anyway, I saw his face and realized it was one of the missing younglings. I thought maybe I misjudged what he was doing since he broke away from the woman and walked into this alley, but he knew I was following him," I explained, troubled by what had occurred. "It was a trap in a way. He came at me."

"That makes no sense," he said, head tilting slightly. "The Summer fae do not attack humans."

"Yeah, well, he attacked me and I did nothing to instigate it either." There was something pecking away at the fringes of my thoughts. "Wait a second. Elliot said some weird stuff. He said his parents weren't his parents any longer and he also called them wannabe humans."

"Did he say anything else?" he demanded.

I shook my head as I saw Elliot's face in my mind. "But his eyes were messed up."

"What do you mean?"

"They were pitch black, like I couldn't even see the irises...." I trailed off as I thought about his eyes. "I've never seen anything like that, but...."

He stepped toward me, voice low. "Are you positive that is what you saw?"

"Yes. He was this close to my face." I put my hand within kissing distance of my face to show him. "His eyes were all black."

The Prince's jaw hardened as he looked away.

There was a sudden feeling where I felt like I'd seen something or a reference to eyes like that before, but I couldn't place it. Like a word that rose to the tip of your tongue, but you couldn't quite grasp it. "Do you... do you know what could cause that?"

"I don't—" The Prince's head swung sharply to the left and then a curse exploded out from him. He moved toward me just as a shot rang out, echoing through the alley.

Chapter 16

The Prince crashed into me, taking me to the ground before I had a chance to see who was shooting at us. I had only a moment to prepare myself for the bone-shaking impact with the ground, but that never came.

Somehow, he shifted at the final second, taking the brunt of the fall. He hit the ground hard, my front plastered to his long length for about a heartbeat and then he rolled suddenly, shoving me under his body as the cracks of a gun firing went off again—and again. My entire body jerked in surprise as a bullet hit the ground right beside our heads, sending tiny pieces of gravel into the air.

The Prince lifted his head and those near transparent eyes locked onto mine. "Stay down," he ordered.

"W-What?"

Launching to his feet, he spun around and then he was no longer there, moving so fast I couldn't track him in the shadowy alley.

I flipped onto my belly, lifting my head as I kept low to the ground. I was going to stay down, because I really didn't want to get hit. Another shot rang out and then I heard a grunt as my gaze swung to the back of the alley.

Two large forms collided. There was a flash of reddish-yellow glow coming from the hands of the Prince, a circular flash of light that reminded me of a fire ball. And then the smell of burnt metal filled the air a second before one of the bodies flew back several feet, slamming into the building opposite me.

The body fell forward into the dim light. My eyes widened as I saw that it was a fae. That... that was uncommon.

They rarely used guns, but unless a human had doused themselves in silver paint and had their ears shaved into points, that was definitely a fae.

The Prince tossed the ruined gun aside, and I knew he'd been the source of the burnt scent of metal. He'd done something to that gun.

Dear God, that kind of power....

He prowled forward like a caged animal finally unleashed, his chin dipped low, and I swore those pale eyes were glowing. "Who sent you?" he demanded, his voice a deadly growl that sent a wave of shivers through me. "Was it Aric?"

Struggling to his feet, the fae swayed as he reached into his boot. I tensed, expecting him to whip out another gun.

I was wrong.

It was an iron stake.

The fae grabbed it with his bare hand. He hissed in pain, lips peeling back in a snarl as he straightened.

The Prince shot forward. "Don't—"

Too late.

Slamming the business end of the stake into the center of his chest, the fae ended it right then and there. Within a few short seconds the fae who'd shot at us was gone.

"Holy shit," I whispered, raising unsteadily to my feet. "Did that just happen?"

"Yes." The Prince was suddenly in front of me, causing me to jerk back a step. His expression was drawn and tight. "Are you okay?"

"Yes. I think so." I felt myself up, searching for holes that shouldn't be there. "What the hell just happened?"

"I do believe we were being shot at."

Hands stilling, I lifted my gaze back to his. "Gee. Really? Let me clarify my question. Why do you think a fae shot at us and then sent his sniper ass back to the Otherworld? That doesn't happen every day."

"It doesn't?"

"No. Not in my world. It happens in yours?"

"I've made a lot of enemies, sunshine. A lot who'd rather see me return to who I was," he said, and my chest squeezed at the mere mention of him returning to the Prince who was an absolute nightmare. "Or see me dead."

"That's kind of scary—" Gasping, I jerked my hand away from my stomach. It was wet, and even in the poor lighting, I could see the dark smudges. "There's blood on my hand."

"You said you were okay." One hand was suddenly wrapped around my wrist while the other was on my stomach, pressing.

"Hey!" I smacked at his hand, but he studiously ignored me. "I don't think I'm bleeding." When he still felt along my midsection, I caught his hand and squeezed hard. "I think it's your blood."

"I'm fine," he gruffed out. "Are you sure you haven't been hit?"

"Pretty sure I'd know if I'd been shot," I said, squinting at him. He was wearing a dark thermal and pants, like he had the first time I'd seen him. I placed my hand on his right shoulder and felt nothing. I slid my hand down his chest, and he sucked in a sharp breath.

"What are you doing?" he asked, voice deeper, thicker.

My gaze lifted to his, and I thought I probably should pull my hand away, but I didn't. I moved to the other pec, and it was me who sucked in air this time. Wet warmth hit my palm. "You've been shot."

"It's nothing."

"Nothing?" I exclaimed. He let go of my wrist, so I got both hands involved. "You've been shot in the shoulder, too!"

The Prince said nothing.

I didn't know the biology of Ancients, but I figured, like the fae, they could survive mortal wounds. But a chest and shoulder wound? I stepped back, lowering my hands and wiping them over my jeans. Did the pant leg of his right thigh look darker? Shot three times? That... that was a lot.

My stomach pitched with concern I probably shouldn't feel, but he *had* covered my body with his when shots rung out and he *had* paid for the crab cakes and crawfish.

"We need to get out of here," I said, looking over my shoulder, to the entrance of the alley. "With that many gunshots, police will be on their way. Can you heal yourself?"

"Normally." His voice was off. Not like it had been when I'd been feeling him up or Monday night, but there was something strained about it. "You should get out of here before the police arrive."

Or more gun toting fae showed up since this was apparently an everyday occurrence to him. "What do you mean by normally?"

"Do you always ask this many questions?" he demanded.

"Yes. Is it annoying?"

"Yes," he growled.

"Sorry, but you're going to have to deal with it," I shot back.

He'd moved back into the shadows, but I could practically feel his glare. "You know that the fae can heal from virtually any wound if they feed," he said.

And rather quickly too. That's what made fighting them so dangerous. You didn't have a lot of time for what they'd consider flesh wounds.

"I know that, so you should...." Understanding dawned. "You... you need to feed?"

He let out a dry, racking laugh. "Something like that."

"When was the last time you... you fed?" Those words sickened me, and a part of me didn't want to know the answer.

"A while."

I stared at him for what felt like a whole minute. "What exactly does 'a while' mean? A couple of days? A week?"

"Try longer than that."

A frown pulled at my lips. "Longer than a couple of weeks?"

That didn't make sense to me, especially with him being at a place like The Court where humans were happily on the menu.

He said nothing.

"A month? A couple of months?" I whispered. Knowing what I did about the fae, they had to feed on a regular basis to slow down the aging process and give them their preternatural abilities. The Prince might look like he was in his mid to late twenties, but he had to be hundreds of years old, if not older. The fae metabolism was much like ours. They might not need three square human meals a day, but from the Order's research, they had to feed at least once every other day.

"You need to go," he said as the faint sound of sirens could be heard.

"And leave you here to bleed all over yourself, the alley, and perhaps even on police officers?"

"Do you really care what happens to me?"

My fingers twitched. "No."

"Then *go*." He started to back up.

I should go. I should leave his ass here to bleed out like a stuck pig. He was an Ancient, and even if he hadn't fed in a few months....

Holy crap.

It struck me then. "You haven't fed this whole time, have you? Not since the spell was broken."

He tossed a glare at me over his shoulder through thin slits. "Aren't you leaving?"

"What does that mean then if you haven't fed in like two years? Can these wounds—"

"Kill me unless it's treated or I feed? Probably not, but it'll take a while to heal." Grunting, he pushed against the hole in his shoulder. "I just need to get out of this alley."

"You can't go to the hospital." Having a very human doctor discover that fae were a real thing was not exactly on the to-do list for tonight.

"No shit," he grumbled.

I ignored that. "I can—I can get you back to Hotel Good—"

"No," he interrupted, and I thought that he might've swayed a little. "You will not contact them."

Confusion filled me. "What? Why?"

"Can you just accept an answer without following up with another damn question?" He let out another curse. "God, you're infuriating."

I lifted an eyebrow at that. "You know, if I am so infuriating, then you probably shouldn't have stalked me into the alley."

"I wasn't stalking you," he grumbled. "And if I hadn't been then you'd have ended up dead."

I threw up my hands. "First off, you just admitted to stalking me after saying you didn't, and we'll address that, but most importantly? I'm not the one bleeding all over myself, now am I?"

He didn't respond to that, at least not vocally, but I had a feeling he was mentally cursing me out.

"I'm fine. I just... I just need to get to my place," he said, and he sounded like those words pained him.

The sirens were getting closer, and I needed to make up my mind. He needed help, whether he wanted it or not.

Taking a deep breath, I walked over to where he stood and decided. "Like it or not, I'm going to help you."

* * * *

There weren't a lot of moments in my life where I had to stop and ask myself what in the fuck I was doing.

For the most part, I lived a practical, boring existence—well, outside of my plan to hunt down the fae who'd attacked my mother and me. Other than that, I was like a bowl of white rice without any soy sauce.

But here I was, waiting for the Prince—*the* Prince—to unlock the door to what appeared to be one of the many old warehouses that had been converted into upscale condos.

Luckily he hadn't argued with me when I'd led him out of the alley, and I was leading him. By the time we reached Royal Street, in the opposite direction of the sirens, his steps had slowed to a near crawl. I was able to flag down a cab and thank God, as far as I knew, he didn't bleed all over the backseat.

The Prince didn't speak beyond giving the cabbie his address. Not again after the ride. Not as I helped him get to the elevator and we went to the tenth floor, the top floor, and not as I stood beside him, shouldering what felt like the weight of a Volkswagen Bug.

The door finally opened and warm air rushed out as the Prince stumbled inside. A light came on, revealing a massive open floor design that… that didn't even look lived in.

The walls were exposed brick and the living area faced floor to ceiling windows. There were two doors. One near the entrance that I figured was some kind of closet and the other on the other side of the living room. There was a TV and a large black, sectional couch, but beyond that, there was nothing else. At all.

"You can leave now." He walked forward, stopping to place his hand on the white marble countertops that edged out the gourmet level kitchen that looked like it never once saw a meal cooked in it.

Because I was apparently making a series of bad life choices tonight, I followed him inside, closing the door behind me.

"Are you going to be okay?" I toyed with the button on my peacoat.

Lowering his head, he let out a long, shuddering breath. "Yes."

"That doesn't sound very convincing." I inched closer to him, and I could smell it now. It mingled with that summer scent of his. I saw it on his hand, the bluish-red tint of fae blood. "Is there someone I can call? Your brother—"

"Do not call my brother," he bit out, his fingers curling into a fist on the marble. "Do not call anyone."

Exasperated, I looked around the condo before my eyes settled on him. "Obviously you're not okay. You haven't fed and you're bleeding all over your nice wood floors. And I have no idea why you haven't fed in two years—not that I don't think that's great and all, but your brother says he uses human *volunteers*—"

"You say that like you don't believe it, but yes, my brother does not take from those who are not willing."

"And you couldn't find any volunteers?"

"There you go again, with the questions." He shook his head slowly. "You need to leave."

"But—"

"I do not think you understand." He lifted his head again, and yep, those eyes were definitely starting to glow. He stared at me like... like he was *hungry*. Starved, really. "You need to leave now."

A wave of shivers rolled over my skin as an innate sense forced me to take a step back from him. The atmosphere around us seemed to thin and charge with static.

The Prince turned, tracking my movements with a near predatory glint to those glowing faint blue eyes. "I won't tell you again. If you don't leave, you won't have the choice to."

Chapter 17

He didn't have to tell me again.

I got out of that condo as fast as my two legs would carry me and I made it down the long hall, to the steel elevator doors before I stopped and looked behind me.

"What are you doing?" I whispered, knowing I should just hit the elevator button and go. He wasn't my responsibility and just because I could appreciate his hotness didn't mean I liked him.

Because I didn't.

I stared at the elevator button.

Plus I had to figure out what the hell I was going to tell Tanner and Faye about Elliot and his weird as hell eyes. It would take Faye no leap of logic to jump to the conclusion that if Elliot had gone all evil fae, there was a good chance her cousin had too.

Turning from the elevator, I pulled my phone out of my back pocket. "Damn it," I muttered, folding one arm across my stomach as I called Tink.

He answered on the second ring. "Hey, Lite Bright, I was getting worried."

"I'm okay, but there is a problem." I glanced up the hall. "I'm with the Prince."

There was a pause and then, "Like *the* Prince?"

"Yes."

"As in Fabian's brother?"

"Yes, Tink, unless there are other Princes I'm unaware of."

"Why are you with him?" Tink demanded. "Oh my God, did you

really have a date tonight and then lied about looking for younglings? Oh, my God, you *hussy*."

"Tink—"

"Hussy Brighton got good taste, though. Hold on, I need popcorn for this conversation."

"Tink," I snapped. "Come on, I'm not on a date with him and you don't need popcorn for this conversation. I was out looking for the youngling and I ran into the Prince." I figured I'd leave the whole Elliot part out at the moment. "He was shot multiple times."

"Oh, dear."

"Yeah, and he's in pretty bad shape. He didn't want me to call his brother or anyone from Hotel Good Fae."

"You just called me," he pointed out.

"I know that." Exasperated, I closed my eyes and kept my voice low. "I called because he's in bad shape and he hasn't fed."

"He should still be okay. Probably needs to sleep it off—"

"He hasn't fed in two years," I cut him off.

"What?" Tink shrieked. "Are you serious right now? I need to call Fabian—"

"Don't call him. He asked me not to." I had no idea why I was following his orders. "Look, is he going to be okay or not?"

"No, Lite Bright, he is not going to be okay!" Tink yelled, and my stomach sunk. "If he hasn't fed in two years, he's basically mortal except it's just going to take him longer to die!"

"Crap," I muttered, turning back toward the Prince's door. "Well, this sucks, because he's alone at his place, and I'm not sure I can lure a human back for him to snack on."

"You can feed him."

"What?" I almost dropped the phone. "Are you out of your mind?"

"It's not a big deal. Trust me. You'll probably like it."

My mouth dropped open.

"Brighton, he can't die. Do you understand me? If he doesn't feed, he will die and if he dies…."

"He'll be dead?" Screw this. "Go ahead and call his brother. I don't care if he gets pissed at me. I'm—"

"There's no time to call Fabian. He'll be dead by the time Fabian can get to him. You either need to offer yourself up as an all you can eat buffet of Brighton or you need to go kidnap some person and serve him up a dish of unwilling human."

I had no words.

"And considering his background and all the terrible shit he knows he's done while under the Queen's spell, I'm sure he'll be down for that," Tink continued on.

There was another pitch to my stomach. "That sucks, but this isn't my problem."

"You called me, so obviously you think it's your problem."

He had me there.

"He can't die," Tink said into the phone, his voice more serious than I'd ever heard him before. "If he dies, then the entire Summer Court will be weakened."

I started to say that also wasn't my problem, but it kind of was. When the Queen came back, because she would, the Order and the world would need the Summer Court at full power.

"And if he dies, then Fabian becomes King and he... he can't be King, Brighton." Tink's voice had dropped to a whisper. "If you can't help him, then I will."

"You helping him means you're going to kidnap someone." I turned, dragging my hand over my head. Crap! I hated my life. "I'll take care of it."

"Will you?" Tink asked. "Because like the entire Court and the world rests on you taking care of this."

I rolled my eyes. "Are you not at all worried he's going to suck me dry?"

"No." He was so quick to answer that I frowned so hard it was no wonder it didn't break my face. "He would never hurt you, Brighton. Never."

My face smoothed out as surprise rippled through me. It took me a second to even formulate a decent response. "Why would you even say that? You don't know that."

"I do know, because it's true." Tink took a big enough breath that I could hear it through the phone. "The Prince wouldn't hurt you. Not when he already saved your life once before."

"What?" I laughed. "What are you even talking about, Tink?"

"You said I saved your life the night you were attacked, but I didn't save your life, Brighton. I just found you," he said. "But it was the Prince who saved your life in the hospital."

The memory of seeing the Prince suddenly resurfaced as I clutched the phone. I saw him there, but I thought... I thought it had just been some weird trauma or drug induced hallucination.

"You were going to die, Brighton. Too much damage had been done, but he did something. Do you understand?" Tink asked. "He saved your life and now you must save his."

Chapter 18

How does one come to grips with the unexpected knowledge that someone they barely knew, someone who wasn't even human and just happened to be *the* Prince, had not only saved their life but did God knows what to do it?

Part of me couldn't even believe it because as far as I knew, the fae couldn't heal humans. Unless it was something only Ancients could do. But if so, that was yet another thing I was unaware of, and I was *supposed* to be the leading authority on all things fae.

Apparently I didn't know jack.

After promising Tink we were so going to have a conversation about all of this when I got home—*if* I got home—I found myself back at the Prince's front door.

I couldn't even let myself think about what I was doing as I reached out and turned the knob. It was still unlocked.

Saying a quick prayer that, all things considered, would probably go unanswered, I walked back into the quiet condo, closing the door behind me while hoping I was going to walk back out of there.

He saved your life and now you must save his.

This was insane.

What Tink had said was just unbelievable, but I kept walking.

The kitchen was empty and I stopped by the counter, spying a reddish-blue blotch of blood. That was probably going to stain the marble.

I don't know what I was thinking when I walked around to the kitchen sink, picked up a towel and wiped up the blood. Probably because I wasn't thinking at all.

There was no sight or sound of the Prince.

What if he was already dead?

He saved your life....

"Uh... hello?" I called out, tossing the towel into the sink. I eyed the door I figured led to a bedroom. "Uh, Prince? It's me, Brighton?"

Silence.

Concern wiggled around in the pit of my stomach like a nest of vipers. I started toward the bedroom, seeing that the door was ajar. Lifting a trembling hand, I pushed it open. I'd been correct. It was a bedroom and it was as personable as the living room. In other words, it didn't look remotely lived in. Just a super large bed in the middle of the room with deep blue sheets and comforter. There was a nightstand and a dresser. That was all.

Now you must save his....

Light spilled out from a room off from the bedroom and tiny tremors rattled my legs as I stepped farther inside. "Are you in here? Like alive?"

Several beats of silence passed and then, "I told you to leave."

The guttural voice caused my breath to catch in my throat, and I froze.

"And you left." There was another pause. "You should not have come back."

The entire world with the exception of Tink would agree with that statement.

But I was here.

"I know... I know you're not okay." I forced my legs to move, and it was like walking in quicksand. I neared the swath of light. "I know that you're going to be really not okay because you haven't fed."

There was no response.

Wanting to turn and run in the other direction, I did the opposite and stepped into the light.

And I saw him.

"Holy...."

The Prince was... he was shirtless, and while I'd seen a decent number of shirtless men in my life, I'd never seen one like him.

And that had nothing to do with the trails of blood running down his back and stomach, as terrible as that was to admit. My priorities were so, so wrong, because I wasn't checking out the ragged holes in his shoulder or chest. He was....

He was beautiful, even covered in blood.

All that golden, hard skin. Defined pecs. Abs tightly coiled and a dusting of golden hair that traveled below his navel to the band—

Oh, sweet Jesus, his pants were undone and hanging low enough that I could tell the man went commando underneath.

I should look away.

I couldn't look away.

Not when my gaze got hung on those interesting indentions on either side of his hips. How in the world did someone get muscles there? I'd never seen that on someone in real life. Only in photographs or on TV. I was beginning to think those kind of muscles were fake news, but he had them and then some. Actually, his body was absolutely freaking glorious, and it was clear that I needed to obtain sexual gratification from anything other than my trusty vibrator, because I was staring at him like I'd never seen a man before and—

"Do you like what you see?" he asked.

Jerking my gaze to his, I felt heat blast my face as I blurted out the stupidest thing possible. "You're bleeding."

The Prince tilted his head to the side as he held a bloodied towel in his hand. "I was completely... unaware of this."

A thousand smartass responses traveled to the tip of my tongue and died there, because he turned to the gray and black tiled shower stall. Muscles flexed and contracted as he tossed the towel into the stall.

"You have to know why I told you... to leave," he was saying, twisting at the waist and gripping the basin of the sink so tightly his knuckles bleached white. "I will be fine."

He saved my life? How?

He had to have, because why would Tink lie? And I knew I should've died that night. The pain and all that blood and the scars... the scars no one but those doctors have seen.

The Prince saved my life.

And not only that, he understood why I had to do what I had to do. He didn't like it. He made it more than clear he didn't want me to do it and now a lot of what he'd said made sense, but he still understood.

No one understood.

I'd never let anyone in the last two years get a chance to understand. Not even Ivy, but I let... I let the Prince in and I was now just realizing that. I'd let him in and even though I knew of him for two years, I'd only *really* known him for a week. And he already knew more about me than most.

What did that mean?

Something warm and confusing and consuming filled up my chest as I stared at this beautiful, complicated *man*. And that's what I saw when I stared at him. Not a fae. Not an Ancient. Not a Prince. Just a man.

A man who was dying.

And I could save him.

"No, you won't be okay." I found my voice and actually said something useful. "I know if you... if you don't feed, you will die."

His gaze swung to mine and his features were sharper, more stark. He took a deep breath and it lifted his chest. "Are you... offering yourself up?"

My heart stuttered in my chest as he pushed away from the sink and faced me. "I'm here and I really can't believe I'm here, but it's either me or I go out and kidnap a human, and the latter isn't going to happen."

His bloodied hands opened and closed at his sides. "I am not going to feed from you, Brighton."

"Then you're going to die."

A muscle flexed in his jaw and a moment passed. "You do not want me to feed from you."

"Not particularly," I admitted. I'd never been fed on before. Not even when I'd been attacked, but I knew what feedings could do. I could walk out of here like nothing happened or he could take too much.

He took a step toward me, and I tensed. His nostrils flared. "Then why are you here, offering yourself to me?"

I could lie, claim that I was an altruistic soul, but I had feeling he'd know that was utter crap.

"Because I... I know." I swallowed hard, meeting his gaze. Those eyes burned straight into me. "I don't understand how and I don't understand why, but I know you saved my life."

The Prince became very still, so much so that I feared for a moment he'd died right there and was about to topple over, but when he didn't, I continued.

"I thought I saw you in the hospital, but I wasn't sure. You were there and you did something to make sure I pulled through." Now my heart was pounding fast, too fast. "That's why the doctors said I was a miracle. Because I was."

The Prince closed his eyes.

I wanted to ask him why, but we'd already wasted too much time. Hopefully there'd be a chance to find out later.

"You saved my life, so I'm going to return the favor," I said, stepping back.

His eyes snapped open. "That's not why I did it. So you could return the favor."

"Well, I would hope not." I kept walking backward, relieved when he followed me like an animal stalking its prey. Probably not the best comparison to make at the moment.

The back of my legs hit the bed at the same moment I figured it out. "You saved me because I helped your brother the night everyone fought the Queen."

His head tilted to the side and he didn't answer. He didn't need to.

I knew.

Reaching into the pocket of my peacoat, I pulled the stake out and placed it on the dresser. "So, I, um, don't accidentally stab myself or you."

His chest was rising and falling rapidly as he watched me.

Nervousness nearly made my knees shake as I fiddled with my jacket. Then I undid the button, thinking it was too hot in this room. I shrugged off the ruined peacoat, letting it fall to the floor.

The jeans and the light, loose sweater still felt like too much, but I wasn't going to strip. "I'm not going to leave, Mr. Prince, and I'm not going to let you die."

In a blink of an eye, he was right in front of me. Caught off guard, I lost my balance and sat down on the edge of the bed.

"Do you know what will happen when I feed?" His voice was barely above a growl.

Staring up at him, I swallowed. "I know... I know some people like it... or so I've heard, but I guess...no, I really have no idea."

"You're going to like it."

A wholly unexpected thing happened. Heat boiled my blood. "I wouldn't go that far."

He stared at me for a long moment. "You have no idea what you're getting yourself into."

"I know what I'm getting myself into."

The Prince's hands moved faster than my eyes could track. His fingertips touched my cheeks. "You can leave."

"If I do then you die."

"Maybe that's for the best."

Stunned and more than a little disturbed, I lifted my hands and wrapped them around his wrists. "Why would you say that?"

He was getting paler by the second. Soon he'd be as white as a ghost. "You know what I've done."

"It wasn't your fault."

"There is no coming back from that."

"Stop," I said, my voice cracking. "You have come back from that, because you're standing here and you're going to feed so you don't die. That's it. This has been decided. Get with it."

He went still, but I saw the moment resignation settled into his features. Relief mingled with a little bit of fear. He was going to live, and I just hoped I didn't die in the process.

"I won't hurt you," he whispered. "And I won't let this go too far. I promise you this."

Before I could ask what too far meant, the tips of his fingers glided down my cheeks, along the sides of my throat. He tilted my head back and a heartbeat passed.

"I didn't save you because of what you did for my brother," he said, and then he brought his lips down.

Chapter 19

The Prince didn't kiss me. He didn't move his lips against mine. It was the lightest touch, and I still felt the contact in every cell, in every part of my body.

And then he exhaled against my lips.

It was like warm silk slipped down my throat and it tasted like sun-baked coconut. How strange was that? The warmth hooked itself into the very center of my being and then *pulled*.

My entire body jerked as if I too was being lifted, but I wasn't sure if I actually moved or not or if the Prince was holding me in place when his hands glided down to my shoulders.

It didn't... it didn't hurt.

Not at all. Instead, I felt... lighter. Like I was floating in warm water. The warmth from his body blanketed my skin, and I was only vaguely aware of my hands slipping off his wrists, to fall to my sides. But when he tilted his head to the side, the deep, deep tugging intensified and then—oh, God—then it turned into something else.

Everything inside me tightened all of a sudden. My heart raced as my senses overloaded. A rush of acute pleasure came out of nowhere, slamming into me with a force that turned my blood to nothing more than liquid heat as a coiling sensation began deep inside me. There was no stopping the sound that came out of me as my entire body arched—a sound that I knew I would be mortified about later.

The Prince shuddered as his hands curled under my arms. He lifted me up and then laid me down and then his weight came down on me.

I stopped thinking.

I stopped being me, whoever me was, and I just let what I was feeling happen, and what I was feeling was something so beautiful it was almost painful.

My hands slid to the bare skin of his chest and my legs spread as his thigh eased between them. My body wasn't my own, and I didn't care. I began to move, twisting and churning against his thigh, the friction so good it made me pant. One of his hands curved around my hip as he braced his weight on his other.

And then it happened.

The whirling force inside me whipped out of control as the first wave of pure, full-bodied bliss crashed over me. I cried out against his mouth as spasms racked my body, and it went on and on, a wave I rode for what felt like an eternity. When it was over, every muscle in my body was limp.

I only became aware as the soft tugging motion slowed, eased and then faded off. He wasn't feeding anymore, but his mouth was still close to mine and the pounding in my chest had turned to a throbbing in several pulse points throughout my body. That delicious ache was still there, pulsing, pounding, waiting for *more*, because while the experience had been amazing, there was this hollowness about what I'd just felt. And I knew it was from him feeding and I knew it was... it was simply because it was *him*.

The Prince lifted his head.

I opened my eyes and saw that his were closed. His head was thrown back, neck muscles taut and corded. He was striking like this, awe-inspiring. I lowered my gaze to his shoulder. The wound was healed, as was the one in his chest. Nothing but faint streaks of dried blood remained. I figured the one in his thigh was also healed, but he looked like he was... he was in pain.

I lifted my hand, placing just the tips of my fingers onto his cheek. "Are you... you okay?" When he didn't answer, I guided his chin down. "Prince?"

His chest rose with a sharp, unsteady breath and when he opened his eyes, I gasped. Their color had changed.

"Your eyes," I whispered. No longer were they the pale wolf's blue. Instead, they were a stunning shade of amber, rich and intense.

"It's all right," he said, voice thick. "It was... it was bound to happen."

My brows knitted. "What... what does that mean?"

He gave a little shake of his head. "Nothing. Are you okay?"

I managed a nod.

Those eyes drifted shut again. "Can you do me a favor?" He turned to my hand, startling me when he kissed the center of my palm. "Call me Caden."

"Caden?"

"That is my name." His lips brushed my palm again. "My name is Caden."

A swelling sensation rose in my chest. "Okay. Caden. I can do that." I lowered my hand to his bare shoulder and he flinched. I jerked my hand away. "Are you sure you're okay? Did you take enough?"

"Did I take enough?" He let out a dry laugh as he dropped his chin to the chest. "I took enough."

"Then what's...?" Air caught in my throat as the Prince—no, as *Caden* shifted just an inch, pressing against me, and I felt him then, hard and heavy against my hip.

He was aroused.

Seriously so.

Those odd eyes were closed again and those features were just as stark as they had been before he fed. He was hungry... he was hungry for *me*.

I don't know what it was. If it was what we just shared that gave me the courage or if it was something deeper than that, but whatever it was, I welcomed it.

Grazing his cheek with my fingertips, I dragged my thumb over his full bottom lip, reveling in the way he inhaled sharply, as if my touch had some heavy impact on him. My thumb followed the line of his jaw and his eyes drifted shut as the muscle along his jaw flexed against my palm.

"What are you doing?" he asked.

"I don't know." That wasn't completely true. I knew what I was doing as I threaded my fingers through the silky soft strands of hair and curled my hand around the nape of his neck, tugging his head down as I lifted mine.

I knew exactly what I was doing when I brushed my lips over his parted ones, touching the tip of his tongue with mine.

Caden locked up. He didn't move. He didn't kiss me back. He just froze above me, and when I opened my eyes, his were wide and dilated.

Oh no....

Had I done it... wrong? It had been forever since I'd been kissed and even longer since I kissed someone, so I had no idea if I was doing this right or if there really was a wrong way of doing this.

I started to pull my hand away. "I'm—"

His hand left my hip and shot to my neck just as his mouth came down, stopping a hairsbreadth from touching mine. "We can't." His thumb smoothed over my wildly beating pulse. "We can't do this."

Confusion filled me. "We can't?"

Caden shuddered as he dropped his forehead to mine, his hips moving in a slow roll.

"No."

"No?" I whispered.

"I promised you that I would not let this go too far."

"I want this." To prove my point, I ran my hands down the tense muscles of his back and then lower, slipping my fingers under his loose pants. "Don't... don't you want this? It seems like you do."

"God," he groaned, moving his mouth to my neck. "I've never wanted anyone as much as I want you." He kissed the spot just below my ear, causing my back to arch. "But you can't say what you want is all yours. Not after me feeding."

"It feels like it's all me," I said, and I thought I felt him smile against my neck.

"I'm trying to be... better than who I was," he explained after a long moment. He lifted his head and that striking gaze latched onto mine. "I don't know if that will make a difference or mean anything, but I'm trying to be better and it's never been harder than this moment."

My breath caught as I slid my hand back along his jaw and I remembered what he'd said before he fed. That there were some things you couldn't come back from. I searched his gaze as a knot of emotion formed in my throat. I could understand that feeling—that there were some things in life, even if you weren't responsible, you just couldn't get past.

But I didn't... I didn't want that for him. "You aren't guilty for those things you did when you were under the Queen's spell." I caught his gaze when he started to look away. "You're already better. You didn't hurt me. You don't want to take advantage of me. You've saved my life, more than once. You're not him."

He was quiet for a long moment. "Knowing I didn't have control doesn't erase the memories. I was aware of everything, but I couldn't... I couldn't stop myself. I couldn't stop any of it."

My heart squeezed with sympathy. "I'm sorry, Caden. I really am."

His eyes flared wide and then he rolled off me, onto his back beside me. "You're really making this hard."

I bit down on my lip as I stared up at the vaulted ceiling of his bedroom. "Sorry?"

He didn't respond.

It took a surprising amount of energy for me to roll onto my side, but I managed to do it.

"Does your brother know you hadn't fed?"

"I think he's had his suspicions, but he's left it alone."

"Why haven't you fed? Are you wanting to live your life like Tanner?"

"We don't have that choice. If an Ancient doesn't feed, we just weaken and we age, but it's still at a substantially slower rate than humans. Wounds can become mortal and we lose our strength," he explained.

"So, why?"

His hands came to rest on his chest. "When I was under the Queen's control, my feeding was... gluttonous. Several times a day. Some I killed," he said quietly, and I flinched. "Some I enslaved. Others I have no idea what happened to them, and I didn't care. That wasn't the only aspect of my life that became... excessive."

"Sex?" I asked.

"I haven't fed and I haven't been with anyone since Fabian broke the spell. I just...."

I reached over, placing my hand on his arm. "It's okay. I understand."

He turned his head toward me. "You do, don't you, sunshine?"

"Yeah." At least I did on some level. I lowered my gaze to where my hand rested on his arm. "Why do you call me that? Sunshine?"

"Because I saw you smile once and it was like the sun finally rising."

That was... that was *wow*.

"And your hair is like golden rays of sun," he finished.

I laughed. I couldn't help it or stop it. The laugh just came right out of me.

He lifted a brow as a small grin played at the corners of his lips. "I just complimented you and you laughed at me."

"I did. I'm sorry. It's just... it's just coming from anyone but you that would sound ridiculous."

"And it doesn't sound ridiculous coming from me?"

"No," I admitted, lifting my gaze to his. "It doesn't."

That small grin appeared once more. It wasn't a lot, but it was a big deal, I realized.

"I... I have another question."

"Of course you do," he replied wryly.

I grinned at that. "How... how did you heal me? I didn't know that anything like that was possible."

"It's something only I can do."

"Why?"

The Prince sighed heavily, but there was a fondness to the sound, like my one hundred and one questions amused him more than they irritated him. "As the eldest of my Court, I can... how do I explain this? Reverse feed."

"Reverse feed? That sounds... weird."

"Instead of taking from a human, I can give. And if there is still life left in the human, there's a chance what I can do can save them."

I considered that. "So, you basically made out with me while I was unconscious in a hospital bed?"

He snorted. "Not quite. I would not do that. Who I was, though?"

"I know. I was teasing." I squeezed his arm and then started to pull my hand away, but the strangest thing happened.

Caden caught my hand and threaded his fingers through mine. "I did it once before," he said. "When I was under the spell of the Queen and I'd just come through the gateway." Pausing, he exhaled heavily as he turned his gaze back to the ceiling. "Ivy had followed me and we fought. She didn't... fare too well."

I remembered this. That was the night he got his hands on the blood crystal—the crystal that could open the gateway and was now in the hands of the Queen. I'd seen Ivy briefly after the fight and there didn't seem to be an inch of her that hadn't been bruised.

"She was pretty bad off," he said, and he started to loosen his grip, but I held on. His gaze found mine. "I healed her."

"Does she know?"

"Yeah, she does." There was a pause as his lashes lowered. "I think she thought it worked because she was a halfling. I never corrected that assumption."

"Well, thank you... for saving my life."

Those lashes rose. "You don't need to thank me."

"I do. If you hadn't done what you did, I wouldn't be here. I would be—" Unable to stop it, I yawned loudly, flushing at how obnoxious it was. "I'm sorry."

"It's okay." A faint smile reappeared, tugging at his full lips. "It's the feeding. You're going to be really tired for a couple of hours and you'll have the deepest sleep you've probably ever experienced. But when you wake up, it will be like any other time you wake up."

I looked around the room as I started to pull my hand free. It was getting late and the last thing I should do is pass out in his bed. "I should—"

"You should stay."

My gaze swung back to his. "Come again?"

"You can stay."

"I… I don't know." That seemed like a big step toward… toward I didn't know what and I wasn't sure he wanted me here. Yes, he'd saved my life. Yes, he called me sunshine and hadn't taken advantage of me. But he said he wanted me… more than anyone he ever wanted, and that was, well, that couldn't be true.

I didn't think that because I had low self-esteem or anything. I was just realistic. I knew what I was—what I looked like. I also now knew that he hadn't been with anyone in two years. He probably wanted *anything* more than *anyone* at this point.

And that shouldn't matter. It really shouldn't.

But it did nonetheless.

So that meant I really, really should go before I got in over my head when it already felt like I was there.

Tugging my hand free, I went to sit up and it took a moment, but I did it. "I do need to go. Tink will worry."

"Tink." Caden murmured the brownie's name as he sat up much faster and more gracefully than I did. "He's staying with you?"

I nodded as my gaze fell to my ruined jacket. Probably best it stayed here, which meant I wasn't able to take the stake with me. "I guess until Ivy gets back and so does Fabian."

"Do you wonder why he didn't go with my brother?" he asked.

"I have. I asked him why and he said he didn't like Florida. I think he called it the Australia of the United States or something." I reached up and could tell that my ponytail was half undone. I tried to tighten it, but gave up and just pulled the rubber band out.

"I like that."

I glanced over my shoulder at him, and almost wished I hadn't. The golden hue of his skin had returned and as he rose, his muscles did a whole lot of interesting things. "The whole Florida being Australia thing?"

"No. I have no idea if that is true, but I'll take Tink's word on it." He faced me. "I meant your hair. I like it down."

"Oh." My hand floated to the ends of my hair as I shifted my gaze away from his, landed on his chest and decided that was worse, and then I ended up staring at my sneakers. "It's a mess."

"Sunshine," he said, and then his hand was pulling mine away from my hair. He tugged me to my feet. "Still looks like sunshine."

I didn't know what to say to that. "I really need to go."

I thought he'd let go, but when he didn't, I looked up just as he pulled me to his warm chest. His arms went around me, holding me tight, and I... God, I liked that. I can't say I didn't know why I did what I did next. I know why I did, because I wanted to.

Drawing in a shallow breath, I closed my eyes and leaned in, resting my cheek against his chest. When was the last time I was hugged like this? I felt the next breath he took. When was the last time he'd hugged someone like this?

"Thank you," he said, voice rough as he rubbed my back, following the line of my spine. "Thank you for what you did tonight."

"It's no big deal."

He chuckled, the sound untried but nice. "You know that's not true." Pulling back, he dragged those hands up to my cheeks. "Thank you, Brighton."

"You're welcome."

He held me a moment longer as he glided his thumbs over my cheeks, and I thought he might not let go. He might insist that I stay, and if he did, I... would, no matter how much of a bad idea it would be.

But he let go.

Chapter 20

Tink was hanging upside down from my headboard, his wings spread out on either side of him and his little face inches from mine when I woke up.

That summed up how my Saturday morning was going.

"Were you watching me sleep?" I groaned, tugging the comforter up over my head. "Again?"

"I was making sure you were breathing," he answered. "Your chest was barely moving. I was kind of worried."

I rolled onto my side, keeping the comforter over my face. "You didn't seem worried last night when you told me to feed Caden and you weren't even waiting up for me."

"I did wait up for you!" There was a thump near my head that alerted me to Tink dropping down on the pillow. "And I wasn't worried about the—wait, what? Did you just call him Caden?"

Crap. I squeezed my eyes shut. *Caden.* That was his name and there was a flutter deep in my chest that made me want to smile and scream at the same time. "I meant the Prince."

"No, you didn't." A small hand pushed at the back of my head. "What did you do? Did you do more than feed him? Did you feed him with your vag—"

"Oh, my God, Tink, no." Not that I hadn't tried, but I kept that to myself. "And if you weren't worried about me then why did you think I wasn't breathing?"

"You're old. You could've had a heart attack for all I know."

"I'm not old." I ripped the comforter off my head and glared at the little brownie. He was wearing a pair of leather pants, and I had no idea how he got a pair of leather pants in his size nor why he was wearing them. "Jesus, Tink."

"Look, heart disease is the leading cause of death among women—"

"It's not heart disease. I was sleeping. Normally. But then you woke me up."

"Sorry?" He plopped down in front of my face. "So, I'm assuming *Caden* is okay?"

"He is." I wiggled a hand free and scrubbed it down my face. "He's okay. He's going to be okay."

"Good."

Rubbing my eyes, I shifted onto my back. "So, how did you know that he... that he healed me?"

"Fabian told me, and I don't know how Fabian knew. Guessing he told him."

"And you never thought to mention this to me once?"

"How was I supposed to bring that up? Oh, by the way, the Prince saved your life, pass the salt?"

"Actually, yes, you could've brought it up that way."

"It wasn't my secret to tell."

I turned my head toward him. "You did tell the secret."

"Yeah, but I had to. Anyway." Tink leaned forward, cupping his chin in his hands. "So, what happened between you two?"

"Nothing," I sighed.

"Something happened because you're calling him Caden," he pointed out. "And the only person who calls him that is his brother... and now you."

Head still clouded with sleep, I rolled onto my other side, away from Tink. "I need coffee," I told him, throwing the comforter off. "But I need a shower first."

"To wash away the aroma of a really, really good night?"

"Shut up." I tossed my legs off the bed and stood. The room immediately went tipsy turvy and I sat back down. "Whoa."

"You okay?" Tink was in flight, his eyes wide with actual real concern.

"Yeah." I pressed my fingers to my temples. "I just stood up too fast. That's all."

"You should be careful." He placed his hand on my arm. "Take it easy today."

I smiled at him. "I plan to."

His gaze searched my face and then he buzzed off toward the door. "I'll go turn the coffee on."

"Okay. Thank you."

Tink made it to the door and then stopped, facing me. "You do realize how much of a big deal it is that he told you his name?"

Pushing the mess of hair out of my face, I bit down on my lip. The fae were very peculiar when it came to their real names, as were most Otherworld creatures. Obviously, Tink wasn't Tink's real name, just one that Ivy had given him. "Is Caden his real name?"

His wings moved silently as he nodded. "I believe it is an abbreviation of his name, but yes, it is his name. He shared that with you. That means something, Lite Bright."

I opened my mouth, but I didn't know what to say. It didn't matter though. Tink flew out of the room. Did it mean something? I didn't have the answers, and honest to God, my brain was so not ready for a bout of over analyzation.

So, I got up a lot slower and got my butt in the shower. It was somewhere between shampooing and conditioning that I remembered where I'd seen something about black fae eyes.

It was in one of the old books about the history of the fae in New Orleans that Mom had curated over the years, collecting them from retired and deceased Order members. I'd skimmed through them as I shelved them, so I had no idea if it had any useful information, but as soon as I finished showering and towel drying my hair, I changed into a pair of black leggings and a lightweight black tunic-style sweater and decided to find out.

After making a pit stop in the kitchen to grab a cup of coffee, I went back upstairs to the office. The air was stale in the room and particles of dust floated in the beams of sunlight streaming in through the windows, so I flipped on the ceiling fan.

Ignoring the clutter on the desk, I walked to the bookshelves that lined the wall as I sipped my coffee.

There were *a lot* of books and journals, along with personal diaries. Hundreds of them. And I'd almost finished my drink before I found what I was looking for, a worn, forest green leather bound journal marked Roman St. Pierre.

Taking the journal to the chair that sat near the window, I placed my mug on the old chest and tucked my legs under me. I knew who

Roman was. He used to be one of the doctors within the Order and I was pretty sure he'd passed away well over a decade ago. Thumbing past accounts of patrols and random passages about research, I found the section I was looking for.

Dated June 1983 was an entry about a fae who'd been cornered outside an establishment on Decater oddly named… Vanilla. My brows rose at that, but I kept reading and found what I was looking for.

Two male fae were viewed leaving Vanilla and captured a block west. Both appeared to be Changed.

Changed? What the…? I reread that line to make sure I'd read that correctly, and I had.

Their eyes were pitch black, opaque in nature, like the fae that had wounded Torres, confirming Torres' account of the previous attack. Once held in captivity, they experienced rapid degeneration, the likes of which we have not witnessed. Within four hours, there was nothing left of them but dust. Harris believes it was due to their inability to feed, however our previous research suggests that fae can continue living without feeding…

Harris was one of the docs who worked for the Order. Unfortunately he'd died since, so I couldn't call him and ask why in the world a fae would die in that short of a timespan. Or a better question would be what did they mean by infected? I kept reading, turning pages until I reached another entry dated a month later regarding the 'Changed fae'.

"Oh my God," I whispered, nearly dropping the book when I saw her name.

Based on the samples Merle brought back to headquarters, our suspicions concerning the Changed fae were correct. The drink the fae favored had been altered. Trace amounts of an unknown powdery substance similar to Devil's Breath was found in the nightshade. We believe that this substance, which has originated from the Otherworld, is responsible for the Changed fae's increased violent aggression and rapid degeneration. The effects of this substance may be similar to that of Devil's Breath.

Seeing my mom's name caused my chest to compress. It took

several moments before I could continue, but when I did I discovered something quite disturbing.

Several pages had been torn out of the journal in many different places, and there was no other mention of Changed fae or Devil's Breath.

Closing the book, I sat there for a moment. Was that place still there? Vanilla? I didn't think so since I'd never heard of it. Rising from the chair, I hurried over to where the desktop computer sat. It took a Godawful amount of time for me to get to Google since there were about a million update alerts. After an eternity of false leads, I found the location of where I thought Vanilla used to be. Near the Candymaker store, there was now a bar called Thieves. I hadn't heard of the place, but that didn't mean much, because there were a metric crap ton of bars and clubs in and around the Quarter.

Pushing back from the desk, I went to the coffee table, where the stack of maps Mom had of all the secret fae hidey holes were. I spread the maps out, dragging my finger along the old parchment until I found where I was pretty confident Decatur was....

And yep, there was a mark above the location where Thieves was.

"Hell." I straightened, popping my hands on my hips. I probably would've eventually checked out the place, but I hadn't made it that far on Mom's maps.

Wondering what the hell Devil's Breath was, I went back to the computer and typed it in... aaand immediately wished I hadn't.

Devil's Breath was a very real thing, one of the most powerful drugs in the world derived from a *borrachero* tree. It was called scopolamine, South America's zombie drug. When used illegally, it could strip a person's free will, erase their memories, paralyze, and even kill them. Apparently, some doctors prescribed some form of it, for what, I didn't even want to know. But if there was an Otherworld plant similar to this, God only knew what it meant if it could strip the will of a fae—

Well, we already knew what that meant, didn't we? Caden was proof of what could happen when a fae—a very powerful fae—had their free will stripped.

Unsettled by the implications, I started Googling the bar known as Thieves and then moved onto public records such as tax and owner information. Hitting the motherload of information, the unease grew when I saw one of the names.

Marlon St. Cyers.

He was one of the Ancients who'd sided with the Queen and had been a powerful real estate developer. He was deader than dead now, but there was another name listed as the owner.

Rica Car I

That was a strange name. Like so strange the longer I stared at the name on the screen the more I began to think it wasn't an actually name at all but an anagram. An anagram for what?

Grabbing a pen and a notepad, I got down to writing out different variations and it didn't take long for me to come up with a name—a name that was the same for both words.

Aric.

Chapter 21

If Miles was to ever discover what I was about to do, the least of the things that would happen would be me being removed from the Order. The worst? They would treat me as if I'd committed treason, and there'd be no lawyers or a court to hand down punishment. The Order acted as judge and jury, and the penalty for betraying the Order was death.

And I was definitely walking a fine line when it came to acts of treason as I crossed the lobby of the building Caden lived in and hit the button for his floor Saturday afternoon.

I could've gone to Miles with the information I'd discovered, but I wasn't sure he would do anything since it involved missing younglings. If there was something crazy going on with the fae, with them Changing, it wouldn't be a problem the Order needed to deal with.

Yet.

But it could be a huge problem. Because if there was something out there that could strip a fae of their free will, and if that was what had happened to Elliot and the other missing younglings, that meant it could happen to *any* of the Summer fae. Hell, all of them.

And that would be bad. Very bad.

So I was going to Caden, because this concerned him and his court *now*.

As I rode the elevator up, I had no idea if Caden was home or not, but I had no way of getting in contact with him. If he wasn't home then I could either camp out here or go to Tanner or Faye to see if they had a way to contact him.

I wasn't acknowledging that I could've had Tink contact Fabian to get that information. I wasn't acknowledging that, because if I did, then I'd also have to acknowledge that I'd chosen to come to Caden's place, because... because I wanted to see him. And acknowledging that meant also acknowledging that I had taken the time to get changed before I came here. I also brushed my hair and left it down, which was more than I did on most Saturday afternoons, and I was wearing a sweater dress with sensible boots. Obviously, the stretchy royal blue dress was not nearly the sexiest thing I owned, but I always felt good in it.

And I also, *also* wasn't acknowledging why I needed to feel good going to Caden's place.

Heart thumping like I'd run up the stairs instead of taking the elevator, I walked down the hall toward his place, my hand twitching around the strap of my purse. Hand trembling a little, I knocked on his door and then took a step back.

He shared that with you. That means something.

I shoved Tink's words out of my head, and God, this was stupid. I should've just tried to get the number from Fabian. There was no reason for me to come here, especially after what had happened last night. He'd fed and I'd had a full body orgasm, which was freaking lovely, but things would be awkward now. And that was something I should've thought of before I came—

The door opened and there he was, standing before me, looking utterly surprised to see me, but looking really good while being surprised.

Caden was wearing a gray Henley that showed off his well-defined shoulders and chest, and he was actually wearing dark jeans and barefoot.

The man had sexy feet and that was something I never thought I'd think.

I'd never seen him so... normal.

Well, not that he could ever truly look normal, not when his features were so unbelievably pieced together perfectly.

"What are you doing here?" he asked, his voice low.

"Hi." My heart flopped around in my chest. "Sorry to, um, just stop by unannounced, but I've discovered something that..." I trailed off as Caden started to step out in the hallway, about to close the door behind him.

"Who's at the door?" came a voice—a vaguely familiar female

voice.

My gaze shifted beyond Caden as I thought I heard him curse. His doorway opened right up into the kitchen and living room, so I saw her immediately.

At first, I didn't recognize her, because I'd only seen her briefly, and I wasn't expecting to see her again.

Because I was pretty confident that she was dead.

It was the female fae from Flux—the one who had led me to Tobias.

Alyssa.

She was wearing some sort of black sheath dress, one that clung to her lean, graceful figure and showed off the luminous silvery skin and cleavage and legs for days.

Her head tilted to the side as her brows rose. She looked just as surprised to see me as Caden had.

My gaze dropped to her hand. She was holding… a glass of nightshade and she was also barefoot.

Stomach twisting, I took a step back as my gaze swung back to Caden's. He said… he had said that he'd killed the fae who'd been outside the room I'd been in with Tobias, and Alyssa most definitely had been outside.

And now she was here with Caden, dressed in a sexy sheath of a dress, drinking nightshade with an equally barefoot Caden.

The intimacy of what I was so obviously interrupting was just as shocking as seeing Alyssa alive—a Winter fae with the Summer Prince, in his apartment, drinking nightshade.

Shock thundered through me as the pieces were trying to fit themselves together and the stupidest thing entered my head at that moment. *I've never wanted anyone as much as I want you.*

God.

I was so dumb it should be illegal.

"Who is this?" Alyssa asked, drawing closer, her red lips curling up in a curious smile.

Caden's gaze flickered over my face as he arched a brow. "No one."

My entire body jolted as my eyes locked with his. He stared at me like… like he honestly couldn't believe I was standing in front of him.

"That's disappointing." Alyssa was standing behind Caden now, and he tensed when she placed a hand on his upper arm and rubbed. "I thought it was delivery."

Delivery.

As in I was delivering myself as food to them. Dear God. My mind raced through the possibilities. Either everything Caden had told me from the get-go was a lie, including who he'd killed outside Tobias' room and the whole not feeding thing, or I was missing something very important here.

But at the moment, none of that mattered. I needed to get out of here. "I'm sorry," I said, my voice hoarse. "I have the wrong place."

"Obviously." Alyssa smirked as she curled her hand around his arm. "I don't do plain and old."

"Neither do I," Caden added.

I flinched. Wow. That was... that was freaking harsh. I started to turn, because I was this close to attempting to stab both of them.

"Wait." Alyssa stepped around Caden. "Wait a second. Do I know you?"

Shit.

"You look familiar," she said.

Caden turned into the female fae, circling his arm around her slender waist as he laughed. "You don't know her. Come on, there are things we need to get back to."

She was still staring at me. "But—"

Then Caden's mouth was on her neck, and he was saying something too low for me to hear as he guided her back into the apartment. A soft series of giggles erupted from her as he kicked the door closed in my face, without even looking back at me.

* * * *

I stood inside Thieves, nursing a rum and Coke as I scanned the crowded floor. I had no idea what I was looking for, but I was hanging out near the bar, hoping I would see something suspicious. So far, I hadn't even seen a single fae. However, I'd gotten two guys' phone numbers. Two guys who didn't think I was plain and old.

I took another drink, but it did nothing to ease the burn in my chest. Hours later, I still had no idea what I had really been seeing at Caden's place, but whatever it was, it wasn't good.

And that had nothing to do with the stupid, stupid ache in the center of my chest.

He'd lied about who he'd killed at Flux, but there was a tiny logical part of my brain that told me he could be using Alyssa to get to Aric. It was a tiny part, though, because at this point, I could be wrong about that.

Caden obviously lied about killing Alyssa and she would've had to have seen him that night. He could've lied about a lot of things. Like what he was doing looking for Aric. The whole not feeding thing… or having sex, because it sure looked like something was going on there between them.

I flinched. Again. I took another drink. Again.

Scanning the bar, I brushed a strand of long, dark hair over my shoulder. I'd gone home before I came here. Slipping on a long, brown wig, and a sexier, tighter black dress that was shoulder-less.

Ren and Ivy would be back in the next day or so, and I was going to tell them everything—well, I was going to leave out the whole me feeding Caden thing and the full-bodied orgasm, but I had to tell someone about the Prince, because if he was somehow playing for the other team while playing me for shits and giggles, we were screwed.

But that didn't make sense either, whispered that logical voice in my head. He'd killed fae. He'd saved my life. He couldn't be working with the Winter—

A steely, warm arm circled around my waist from behind, drawing me back against a hard chest and stomach. I tensed, preparing to slam my elbow into the stomach of a very inappropriately forward dude.

"What are you doing here?"

Recognizing Caden's voice, I froze sans shoving my elbow into his midsection even though I really wanted to even more now. "Let me go."

His arm tightened. "You didn't answer my question, sunshine."

"Don't call me that," I snapped as I tried to pull free and failed. "And you really need to let me go."

His sigh shuddered through me as he reached around me with his other hand and plucked the drink out of my fingers.

"Hey!"

He placed that on a table beside us and then his hand landed on my sternum, just below my breasts, stopping me before I twisted around to him. "You don't understand what you saw at my place."

"Gee. Really?" I looked around the packed floor, quickly realizing that no one was going to come to my aid. To the casual observer, it looked like he was embracing me. "And how did you find me here?"

The hand below my breasts flattened.

"What in the hell does that mean?" I demanded.

"A byproduct of saving your life. I can easily find you anywhere."

My mouth dropped open. "Are you freaking serious?"

Caden didn't respond, and he didn't need to, because it made sense, how he popped up where I was and how he said he'd know if I went back to The Court.

"Jesus," I muttered. "That's creepy."

He chuckled, and that annoyed me even more.

"It's not funny. And it's something you should've probably given me a heads up on."

"I didn't because I figured you'd have this response."

I placed my hand on the arm that circled my waist. "You need to let go of me."

"And you need to explain to me why you're here."

"Yeah, like that's going to happen now."

"You need to understand what you saw at my place. I wasn't expecting you."

"That much was obvious."

He made a noise that sounded an awful lot like a growl. "I was using her for information on Aric."

"Really? Because I'm pretty sure she's supposed to be dead."

"What?" He pressed his head to the side of mine, and his warm breath danced along my cheek, sending a shiver down my spine. "You need to elaborate on that statement."

"Do I really need to?"

"Yes." His thumb moved along my ribs and then the underswell of my breast. "You do."

My throat dried as my idiotic, lonely body reacted to the slight touch. A different kind of ache settled in my chest. "She was at Flux. She was Tobias's scout."

"I didn't see her when I showed up," he was quick to say. "She didn't even know I was there, but she was seconds from recognizing you, and that would have been bad, sunshine."

"Don't change the subject." My breath hitched as I felt my nipples harden.

"She wasn't there, but I knew she had ties to Aric."

"Am I supposed to believe you?" I demanded. "Really?"

The arm around my waist flexed as his head shifted ever so slightly. His mouth was against my ear. "Have I ever given you reason to not believe me?"

I opened my mouth, but snapped it shut. He hadn't given me reason to think he'd lie. At least as far as I knew.

"I was using her to find out where Aric is laying low at," he continued, and with each word he spoke, his lips brushed the shell of my ear. "She was about as useful as the bullet holes drilled into me yesterday."

"Oh, I don't know about that. Seems like she was pretty useful to you."

"No." His lips touched the spot below my ear. "She was not. Not a damn thing happened between us."

I stared straight ahead, finding myself watching a young man kiss a girl standing next to him.

"Our bodies are closer right now than she and I were," he went on as the couple clutched at one another. "I'm not going to lie to you. She wanted this." The arm at my waist jerked tighter. "She didn't get it."

Closing my eyes, I drew in a shallow breath. "It doesn't matter if she did."

"Yes, it does."

"I don't care."

"That's a lie."

"No, it's not." I turned my head toward his. The edges of his hair tickled my cheek. "I don't care if you did whatever with her. I just care that you're not working with her—working with them."

"If I was working with them then I'm doing a really bad job at it."

"Or a really good job."

He tilted his head down and those damn lips grazed my cheek. "The one person I am working with, or at least trying to, is you."

"The old and plain one?" I shot back before I could stop myself.

"You are neither of those two things." He rested his forehead against my cheek. "And you know that."

My heart launched itself into my throat. "I'm not old."

"No, you're not." It felt like he smiled against my cheek. "And you're not plain. You're the furthest from that."

I didn't respond as I closed my eyes. I could admit to myself in that moment that perhaps I had jumped to some pretty wild conclusions when it came to him working with the Winter fae or doing something shady in that aspect and my... personal issues needed to stay personal.

"I remembered something this morning. I'd seen a reference to those type of eyes before—the all-black eyes that Elliot had." The grip around my waist loosened enough that I was able to pull free and put much-needed space between us. I faced him and saw that he was dressed the way he was when I'd been to his place. "It was referenced in one of the Order journals."

Everything about his expression was alert and focused. "What did you find out?"

He listened intently as I quickly gave him the breakdown, everything from a substance similar to Devil's Breath to who I suspected might own this place.

When I was finished, the line of his jaw had hardened. "I don't know what substance could be used, but that doesn't mean it doesn't exist and I know who owns this place. It's not—" His gaze flicked over my shoulder and a sudden glint filled his eyes. "We've got company."

Caden gripped my hand, hauling me against him. I opened my mouth, but he all but shoved my face in his chest.

"Hi there." Caden's deep voice rumbled through me. "Is this a welcoming party?"

I placed my hands on his waist, listening.

"We want no trouble," someone said.

Caden's large hand dug into my hair, holding my head in place. "I would assume not."

"Neal wants to speak with you."

"Is that so?" There wasn't a response, but Caden then said, "She stays with me."

"He just wants to speak with you."

"And I don't care what he wants," Caden replied. "She stays with me."

There was a pause and then, "Follow us."

Caden shifted so his arm was around my shoulder, but his hand was still at the back of my head, keeping my face hidden. I caught a glimpse of two big males wearing dark shirts. I couldn't see enough of them to figure out if they were fae or not.

We were led to the back of the bar, through a narrow hall and then a door was opened.

"He'll be with you momentarily," one of the males said and then the door closed behind us.

Caden's hand slipped off the back of my head, and I got my first good look at the room. There was a booth and several unopened boxes along the other side of the wall.

"Should we be worried?" I asked, running my hand along the iron cuff.

He turned, eyeing the booth. "Not we. You."

"What?"

"The owner? He's not exactly a friend of mine nor is he a fan of your kind." He knocked back a strand of hair that had fallen forward, grazing his cheek. "And I'm not talking about you being with the Order. He's not a huge fan of humans."

"That's kind of offensive." I glanced at the door.

"Yeah, well, it's too late to get you out of here. If he gets a real good look at you, he'll know you're with the Order."

I started to frown. "How will he know?"

"He just will."

Who was the guy that was coming?

"You're going to have to pretend like you like me."

"I don't know if I can do that." I turned to him.

"Do you think all the fae are as stupid as the three you managed to kill?" He glared at me, and surprised flickered through me. "They will figure it out. This one will definitely figure it out."

I waved him off and started to turn, but the sound of voices on the other side of the door grew close.

"Damn it," he muttered, and then his arm snaked out. Without warning, he slid into the booth, hauling me into his lap. Like legit into his lap, one leg tossed over his, the other curled against the cushion of the chair. The skirt of my dress rucked up, exposing most of my thighs. One wrong move, and my behind would definitely be on display.

Gasping, I immediately planted my hands on his chest and pushed back as I tried to scramble off his lap. We'd been closer than this last night, but this was different, because for some inane, annoying reason, I kept seeing her—Alyssa—with her hand on his arm and his face buried in her neck.

"Stop," he seethed. His arm was like steel around my waist as he tugged me back so I was flush with his chest. His eyes burned with irritation. "You better be really good at acting."

My fingers dug into his shirt. We were way too close. My senses were firing off in every direction, causing my head to spin. His hand slid up my back, sending a wave of acute shivers down my spine.

"Because when the door opens, and he figures out who and what you are, I'm going to have to kill him and then I'm going to be really, irrevocably pissed, because apparently there may be some shit going down here," he continued, curling his hand around the nape of my neck and holding my head in place. "So, sunshine, you better fake it till you make it."

Chapter 22

My face was currently shoved against the Prince's throat. Not that I had much of a choice. His grip was like a vise along the back of my neck, keeping my face hidden.

His thumb smoothed over the tense muscles of my neck, reminding me at that very moment that while he held me in place, his grip was gentle.

Later, I was going to have to examine all my life choices that had led me right to this very moment.

"Keep your face hidden, sunshine." Caden's voice was soft as his other hand landed on my thigh. "No matter what."

The door opened before I had a chance to respond and I heard an unfamiliar voice say, "I was surprised when they said…"

He trailed off, and I imagined it was because he wasn't expecting to see a woman in Caden's lap.

Luckily my face was buried in his neck, because I was sure even with all the makeup on, my face was as red as an overripe tomato.

A throat cleared and then the male said, "This is unexpected."

"Isn't it?" Caden squeezed my thigh as I let out a low growl. "Hope you don't mind. I don't want her getting into trouble."

"I can see where she would get in… a lot of trouble."

I was going to kill the Prince, straight up stab him in the chest with an iron stake. Better yet, I should've just let him die.

A door closed. "So, am I interrupting?"

"Not at all," Caden replied. "Just enjoying an evening snack when you interrupted me."

What in the hell? That comment was so not necessary.

Who I was guessing was Neal let out a low laugh, adding to my irritation. Sliding my hands up and around his shoulders, I dug my fingers into his hair and pulled hard enough that he had to fight the motion of his head jerking back.

Caden's other hand came down on my ass. Hard.

I yelped.

Both males chuckled.

I was going to kill him, so help me God, I was going to—

His hand smoothed over the stinging area and he squeezed. I bit down on my lip as I eased up on his hair. The sting… it burned. Muscles in my thighs tensed as a rush of heat flooded me.

Oh God…. I thought I… I thought I liked that, and that was bad, very bad considering my ass had just been slapped in front of someone.

"Not sure I'd want this one as a snack," Neal replied, and I rolled my eyes.

Caden continued kneading the area with his large hand, and if he thought that was going to make the burn go away, he was wrong. The burn was spreading. "Oh, I plan to keep snacking on this one."

I planned on kneeing him in the junk.

"You wanted to speak with me?" the Prince asked.

"I do." The voice was closer, and then I sensed that he sat at the booth. "I was surprised when I saw you on the security camera. You've been… *back* for two years now and not once have you come here."

"So, is this how you greet all newcomers?" Caden's hand drifted off my rear. That was a good thing—a great thing. At first. Because now his hand was on my bare thigh and his long fingers had slipped under the hem of my dress. My eyes widened. What was he doing?

"Only newcomers like you."

"I feel special," Caden replied.

"You should." There was a pause and then Neal asked, "So, what brought you here after all this time?"

Wanting to see who Caden was talking to, I managed to move an inch, and it was the wrong move because it put me more solidly in his lap. The Prince's hand stilled and tensed, holding me still.

Was he…?

Holy smokes, there was no mistaking the thick, hard ridge straining against my inner thigh.

I did not know what to think about that, but my body… Oh God, *my* body was way on board with what *his* body was doing, and that was wrong, just as wrong as me liking it when he smacked my ass.

"Did you know there were some missing younglings from the Summer Court?" The Prince's thumb began to move again, in a slow, idle slide across my inner thigh.

"I did not, but that is unfortunate to hear," Neal replied. "Do you think they have been here?"

"Possibly. I ran into one of the missing younglings last night. There was something odd about him."

"How so?" Neal sounded bored.

"His eyes were... wrong. So black I couldn't even see a pupil."

"Well, that does sound bizarre."

"Does it?" Caden asked carefully. "You know what's even more bizarre is that there's apparently a substance that can rob a fae of their free will and the substance apparently has a neat little side effect."

"Changes their eye color, I assume?"

I felt Caden nod.

"That is interesting, but I don't see how it has anything to do with my place."

"Do you know what that substance could be?"

There was a pause and then Neal said, "I have never heard of any substance that could have that kind of impact on a fae."

Now that was definitely a lie.

"I have a question for you," Neal said. "Heard through the grapevine that several of my... associates ran into an issue at Flux last weekend."

"They did," he answered, and I tensed. "And you should have better associates."

Wait. If Neal was somehow connected to Tobias, then wouldn't he be connected to Alyssa? I curled my fingers around the neckline of Caden's shirt.

"So, you're the reason why Tobias is no longer among us?" Neal asked, and I was a little surprised that this fae would speak so freely in front of me. He had no idea who I was.

Then again, based on my current position, he probably wasn't worried about what I'd say or do. He probably thought I was glamoured.

"I am," the Prince replied.

He'd just lied.

Holy crap, Caden had just lied for me, and he could've said anything, but he took responsibility for what I'd done. I didn't know how to process that.

Neal snorted. "Tobias was an idiot."

"True." His hand was moving again, and every fiber of my being zeroed in on its travels. "Why would Tobias be meeting with Aric?"

"He was?"

"And you don't know why he was at Flux?"

"I figured he was there to fuck and feed as most do."

I wrinkled my nose.

"And they can't do that here?" Caden asked.

"My establishment is a bit more… high class than that." Neal sighed. "You know, I have heard something else through the grapevine. From what I hear, Aric is wanting to test the loyalty of the fae here."

"Loyalty to the Queen?" he asked, and I sucked in a sharp breath.

Neal didn't answer vocally, but I was assuming he must've nodded, because the Prince asked, "Is Aric planning to find a way to contact the Queen?"

"That is something you'd have to ask him, but if I was a betting man, I would say yes," Neal responded. "Aric wants to be more than a Knight. He wants to be a King."

What the….?

The Prince scoffed at that as his hand crept farther under the dress, those fingers reaching the crease between my thigh and pelvis, causing me to gasp. His other hand squeezed the base of my neck, the touching oddly reassuring.

And that made no sense. So it had to be him. His scent was… it was doing strange things to my common sense, but he smelled amazing. A wicked spice and fresh scent that permeated. The skin of his throat was right there, scant inches from my lips. If I opened my mouth, I could taste him.

I shouldn't be thinking about that. I should be paying attention to this conversation, priorities and all, but he was messing with me, and after what I saw at his place and what I'd done for him, that really ticked me off.

Fake it 'til you make it? Isn't that what he said? Screw that. More like make this just as uncomfortable for him as it was for me. He thought he had the upper hand? He was about to learn that wasn't the case.

"Do you know where Aric—" The Prince's voice cut off abruptly as I flicked my tongue over his skin. The grip on my neck tightened, and

I grinned. He cleared his throat. "Do you know where Aric is staying?"

"I don't." Amusement clouded Neal's voice. "You know that he knows how to stay hidden."

"Unfortunately." The Prince's voice was deeper, rougher. Then I did something I would've never thought I'd ever do. I dragged the tip of my tongue up the side of his neck, and when I felt his chest rise sharply against me, I nipped at his ear. His chest then rubbed against mine, and I wanted to laugh. "There's something I want to know," he said, slipping his hand between my thighs, and the laugh died in my throat. I lost the upper hand that quickly. "Are you still loyal to the Queen?"

The question should've set off a million warning flags, especially since I was still convinced that the name Rica was just an anagram for Aric, but I couldn't think beyond where his hand was, how close his fingers were to *touching* me.

"I was never loyal to the Queen in the first place," Neal answered. "I am not loyal to Aric… or to you."

"I never asked for your loyalty." A moment passed and then he touched me with one finger, dragging it down the silk center of my panties.

I stopped breathing.

"You may not have asked, but don't tell me you don't want it. You're the Summer Court's—"

"I know what I am." His finger toyed with the edges of the panty, grazing sensitive skin. Hazy heat swamped me. I couldn't… I couldn't remember the last time I'd been touched like this. "That does not change that I have never asked for your loyalty nor do I expect it."

"Interesting," Neal murmured. "Can that lovely little morsel in your lap handle both of us?"

Hold up.

Every muscle in my body locked up as I held my breath. I had no idea how the Prince would respond. What if he said yes? If so, things were about to get messy.

"I don't share," the Prince growled.

"Well," Neal drawled. "That's a shame."

Part of me relaxed, but only an infinitely small part that wasn't humming from the swipe of the Prince's fingers. I was breathing heavy, my hands clenching at his shoulders at that sweeping heat. Two years ago I would have never imagined allowing something like this to occur, enjoying something like this.

But I was.

I couldn't lie to myself.

"I'm finding this conversation fairly hard to follow," Neal added, his voice thicker. "And the woman, although disappointingly human, to be rather distracting."

"You and me both," the Prince replied wryly while I wondered if he could feel how damp the thin piece of material was. He had to. So that meant I really would have to murder him. "There's something else I need to ask you."

"Make it quick."

I bit down on my lip as his finger traveled down the center of my panties again, but this time with more pressure. It was no slight butterfly touch. Oh no, this one had purpose. The other hand left my neck and curled around my ass.

"Is Aric partners with you?" the Prince said, and I couldn't stop my reaction as his thumb grazed over the bundle of nerves.

My hips twitched into his hand.

"If he was, wouldn't I know where he is? I just told you that I didn't nor was I loyal to him."

"You did." The Prince turned his head, pressing his hot mouth against my shoulder. The kiss… I don't know. It did everything to me. Startled and confused me. Stirred up the heat and newly discovered lust.

"Are you suggesting what I think you are?" There was a pause. "That I'm lying to you?"

"I'm suggesting that Aric is involved in the missing younglings, because I know the missing males wouldn't have willingly disappeared." His finger moved as he spoke, lingering at the most sensitive spot before traveling along the center. It was driving me crazy. He put the slightest pressure against the crotch of my panties, and I bit down on my lip until I tasted blood to muffle the moan. The Prince still heard it. I knew he did, because he rewarded me with a hard squeeze with his other hand. "Not after so many of them lost family members during the battle with the Queen."

"How many are missing?"

"Four so far." His mouth grazed my shoulder again as the hand on my ass pulled me down and against him—against his erection.

None of this was real. It was all an act. So I gave up and the twitch of my hips turned into a slow, grinding roll. I expected to feel shame and embarrassment, but I only felt desire and need and want.

My hands were moving of their own accord, exploring the dips and planes of his chest and stomach. Blood pounded through my veins as the conversation around me faded out. I was moving now, little rocks and twists, and he was pushing his fingers against me, making me wish there was nothing between his flesh and mine.

And that was *insane*.

I couldn't let myself think about what I was doing—riding his hand as he talked to the fae, flushed and hot and aching. Hell, I couldn't think even if I tried. There was a deep, sharp curl in my core, causing my breath to hitch, and it was different than what I'd felt last night. This was real, but....

It's just an act....

And I needed Neal to leave so we wouldn't have to keep up this act, but I didn't want him to leave, because I was so, so close to release, and I thought... I thought I heard a knock on the door.

"I'll let you know if I hear anything about the younglings." Neal's voice was fading away as I tuned back in.

"I'm counting on that." He swirled his thumb and there was no stopping the moan that slipped up my throat or the way his hips punched up in response. "Neal?"

"Yes."

"If I find out that you have anything to do with the missing Summer younglings or if you've been working with Aric, I will fucking destroy you."

"Understood." There was a pause and then, "Use the room however long you need it."

The door closed, and I was holding my breath again, trembling all over. Caden's fingers stilled against me, but he didn't pull his hand away and I didn't lift my head or jump off him like my legs were made of springs. We both were... waiting, and my heart was thundering, my pulse pounding.

"Do you want me to finish?" he asked, voice coarse and hushed.

Yes.

I wanted him to finish me.

But... what was I doing? Neal was gone and there was no reason for this to continue. No good excuse other than seeking a release from him—from the Prince.

No, not from the Prince. From *Caden*.

He folded his arm around my shoulders as he drew back. His lips moved against my cheek as my chin lowered. "You don't have to say anything, sunshine. You understand?"

I tensed so badly I wondered how I didn't break a bone. Trembling all over, I nodded.

Caden made this sound that should've been frightening, but all it did was set my blood on fire and then his finger was under the thin material, skimming through the dampness and heat. I jerked against his hand. No one—no one had touched me in so long. Years, actually, and I knew then that this was no act.

I shifted, spreading my legs and giving him more access and he took it, smoothing his fingers over me and then inside me. I cried out, letting my head fall back as I lost myself to his touch—to him. My hips began moving again, rocking against his hand. A fierce heat surfaced, overshadowing anything I had ever felt before. Building and building till I feared it would consume me.

And then he did something with his finger, hooking it and finding *that* spot. The tension coiled and then erupted. I came hard, hips bucking against his hand as my forehead dropped against his.

I don't know how long it took for everything that shattered to come back together and the room to come back into focus. When it did, I could feel him hard and throbbing under me.

Maybe it was the pleasant haze of post orgasmic bliss that gave me the courage. I lifted up ever so slightly and reached for the button on his jeans.

"Hey." His voice was soft and thick as he caught my wrist, stilling my hand. "You don't need to do that. What I just did, I did without expecting anything in return."

"I know." My forehead was still resting against his. "But I want to."

He groaned deeply. "I wouldn't be satisfied with your hand or your mouth. I'd want to get inside you and not only is this not the place for that, I sure as hell don't want to be inside you when you look like this. I would want it to be *you*."

I sucked in air, shuddering at his words. No one wanted me for who I was but Caden.

"We need to get out of here." He cradled the back of my neck. "Okay?"

Unsure of how to really process him pumping the brakes on this, whatever this was, I nodded. "Okay."

He drew my head back and then I felt his lips press to my temple.

He kissed me there, and I don't know why, but that act squeezed at my chest like my heart was in a juice grinder. It was sweet and intimate and… It was everything.

Caden helped me to my feet, where I swayed a little as I made sure my wig was in place. He stood and extended his hand. I took it, threading my fingers through his. We both turned—

The door swung open without warning. Standing in the center was the damn female fae. Alyssa. And she wasn't alone. Behind her were two Ancients, and behind them was another.

"That's her," she said, lip curling. "I knew I recognized her. That's the bitch from Flux. The one who went into the room with Tobias."

Chapter 23

"Crap," I muttered.

"You have got to be kidding me." Alyssa sneered as one of the Ancients shoved another dark-haired Ancient forward, into the room. "Are you working with them too, Neal?"

It was that moment when I realized that Neal was an Ancient. He didn't look all that concerned as he faced Alyssa and the other two Ancients, but I was.

There were two bald-headed Ancients eyeing Caden and me like they wanted to rip us limb from limb, and as I eyed Neal, I really didn't trust the Ancient, because I kept seeing the name listed as co-owner.

"I really have no idea what you're talking about and I really don't appreciate being shoved around." Neal lifted a brow. "In my own bar, no less."

Alyssa, wearing the same black sheath, crossed her slender arms. "Do I look like I care?"

"You should," Neal replied, straightening the cuffs of his suit jacket.

The female fae smirked as her gaze flickered from Neal to Caden and then finally to me. "Do you think I didn't know why you were asking about Aric?" she said, speaking to Caden. "You're the Summer Prince. Wasn't like I was going to trust you."

"But you trust Aric?" Caden still held my hand. "You do realize he was one of my Knights before betraying me. Not exactly someone you should trust."

"*Was* being the key word," came a new voice from outside of the hall.

"Hell," Neal muttered.

Caden let go of my hand.

The two Ancients stepped aside as they were joined by another. He came to stand behind Alyssa and....

And my heart—God, it felt like it stopped, because I *recognized* him. I would never forget those high, angular cheeks or close cropped light brown hair. I'd never forget that mouth and the scar that cut through the right side of his upper lip.

"It's him," I whispered, my stomach twisting. I couldn't believe it. The Ancient Caden was looking for was the one who murdered my mother and nearly killed me. I could feel Caden's gaze on me. "It's *him*."

The Ancient's pale-eyed gaze flicked to me as he placed his hands on Alyssa's shoulders. His head cocked to the side. "I remember you." He laughed. "But you looked a hell of a lot different the last time I saw you. Not just the hair and the dress. Less blood."

I reacted without thought. Engaging the iron cuff, I shot forward with a scream of rage.

Caden snagged me around the waist, hauling me back. "That wouldn't be wise."

"Let me go!" I shouted, digging my fingers in his arm. "He killed my mother. He—"

"I get it." Caden's voice was quiet. "I do, but Aric's not yours."

I didn't care what Caden said or how he felt. Aric was mine.

"He knows." Neal crossed his arms. "About the *mortuus* and the younglings."

Alyssa frowned as my stomach sank.

"You son of a bitch," Caden growled, his arm sealing me to him. "You just lied to my face."

Neal lifted a shoulder. "Like I said, I wasn't loyal to you."

"And you said you weren't loyal to him," I spat back.

"You were listening?" Neal chuckled as he looked me up and down. "And here I thought you were... distracted by his hand up your skirt."

"Shut up," I seethed.

"Interesting." Aric glanced between us. "Very interesting, indeed, seeing you with her. A member of the Order. Can't say I'm that surprised. Do you know I've tasted her blood? Just for the fun of it? Kind of like history repeating itself, don't you think? Makes me think of that little bird of yours."

Little bird?

A roar erupted from Caden. He whipped me to the side and then behind him as he charged forward.

"Don't kill her. Not yet. She's very useable." Aric shoved Alyssa forward, and then drifted back as the two bald Ancients went at Caden.

He caught the first by the throat and lifted him several feet off the floor before slamming him down. The impact rattled the boxes as Caden lifted his head, his glare trained on Aric.

Alyssa slinked forward as the other Ancient caught Caden at the waist. Both flew backward, into the booth. Their weight crashed through the table, shattering it.

"He says I can't kill you," Alyssa said, and my gaze flew back to her. "But he didn't say I couldn't hurt you."

She swung on me, but I was ready. There was nothing stopping me from getting to Aric. If I could just take him out, I wouldn't even need to find the last one. *He* would be enough.

Alyssa cursed. "Oh, you're faster than you look."

"Yeah." I popped up behind her. "I am."

She whipped around, throwing out her arm. She caught me across the cheek, spinning me out. Pain burst across my jaw, but I spun back just as she launched herself at me. I threw out my right hand, catching her in the center of her *throat* with the iron stake. Bluish-red spit into the air.

Shock rippled across her face as I smiled. "Good thing no one told me not to kill you."

I yanked my arm to the side, breaking free of bone and tissue. Her head went to one side and her body went to the other.

The Ancient that had tackled Caden went flying across the room and hit the stack of boxes. They toppled to the floor. Bottles clinking off one another and cracking. Liquid poured out as the Ancient dropped to his knees in a mess of broken glass and whiskey.

Neal sighed. "Do you know how much that liquor costs?"

Beside him, Aric smirked at me as he lifted his hand and wiggled his fingers.

A hand clapped down on my shoulder. I swung out, but hit nothing but air as Caden whirled me back behind him. He started forward once more.

Damn it.

My hand closed into a fist, but before I could do anything, I saw movement out of the corner of my eye. The other Ancient was on his feet and in a blink of an eye, he was right in front of me.

I jumped back, but with him, I wasn't quick enough. Gripping the front of my dress, he lifted me up as I shoved my right hand out. He caught my arm as my feet left the floor.

"Crap," I whispered.

Then I was flying.

This was going to hurt.

But I didn't hit the wall. Caden was suddenly there, between me and what most likely would be a whole lot of broken bones. The impact with him knocked the air out of my lungs. Pain burst along my side as he brought me to the floor. Our gazes locked.

"I'm sorry," he whispered, and then pulled back before I had a chance to figure out what he was apologizing for.

Caden spun and spread his arms to the sides. Both Ancients were on their feet, coming between him and Neal and Aric. What the hell was he doing? I started to sit up, inhaling deeply and catching the scent of... the scent of fire and smoke. An orange-yellow aura appeared around Caden, outlining his entire body.

An enormous amount of heat blew backward, lifting the strands of hair from around my face. "What the...?"

The glow intensified until my eyes watered, but I couldn't look away from what I was seeing. A flame licked out from Caden's hand, rippling into the air and spitting sparks as the fire took the shape of a...

A sword.

A freaking *flaming* sword.

With the grace of a dancer, he spun with the sword, and a flash of bright light rippled out as the sword arced high. I caught a glimpse of Neal. His eyes widened as he stumbled a step, backing into the wall. He said something in their native language.

"Well, hell," Aric drawled. "That changes things."

And then the light and heat were too much. Throwing my arm up to shield my eyes, I scooted back against the broken booth. Only when the heat pulled back did I lower my arm and open my eyes.

The two Ancients were dead, heads separated from their bodies, and Caden and I were alone. Aric and Neal were gone.

There was also no sword.

Slowly, Caden turned to me and those eyes of his—the same amber color of the fire—glowed. And as I stared up at him, I had no idea what

I'd just seen, but I knew it was something big.

"You okay?" he asked.

"Yeah." I was still sitting on the floor, arm frozen in the air. "Are you?"

Caden nodded, but as his gaze shifted away from mine and the muscle along his jaw ticked, I didn't think he was telling the truth.

At all.

Chapter 24

"I didn't trust Neal, but I didn't think he would be stupid enough to work with Aric."

I somehow resisted the urge to point out that I had thought the name Rica was suspicious as hell from the moment I saw it as we hurried down Decatur Street.

Caden's hand was wrapped firmly around mine as we cut around groups of people strolling on the street. When we'd left Thieves, I expected everyone to be running screaming from the building since the fight had not been quiet, but when we slipped out the back door, I could hear the conversation from the bar area. Those people had no idea that a fight to the death had just taken place with a freaking flaming sword.

Caden stopped suddenly, beside a sleek black SUV parked a block from Thieves, and opened the passenger door. "Get in."

I looked at the SUV and then at him. "You have a car."

One eyebrow rose. "Is that so surprising?"

"Not as surprising as the flaming sword," I muttered.

He shot me a bland look, and I climbed in and buckled up. I watched him jog around the front of the SUV. He was behind the wheel in seconds, glancing over at me as he hit the ignition button. The moment our gazes connected, they held and I let myself just for a couple of seconds really think about what had just happened.

Who I'd just seen.

"It's him," I whispered as the engine rumbled. "Aric was the Ancient who attacked me and my mother."

Caden reached over and cupped my cheek. He didn't say anything as he drew his thumb along my jaw.

"I can't believe it." A messy, raw knot of emotion formed in my chest. "It was him."

"I'm sorry. I really am," he said quietly. "And I know how badly you want to hunt him down, but you need to stay away from him. I don't say that because I doubt your skill or determination, but he is deadly and he is dangerous. He is as old as me, Brighton, and I'm positive he hasn't spent a day fasting."

A horrible thought occurred to me as his words sunk in. I pulled back. "Did you... did you know it was him?"

"No." He looked away, his gaze flicking to the rear view mirror as he pushed the SUV into reverse. "I'm not surprised. The bastard is sick and cruel, but I did not know."

I wasn't sure if I believed him and I didn't know how to process that right then. I didn't even know how to deal with coming face to face with the Ancient who'd ripped into my mother's throat and torn through my skin while *laughing*.

"We're going to have to involve the Order in this." He eased away from the curb. "With Aric behind the missing younglings and using whatever the hell *mortuus* is, we're going to need all hands on deck."

Hell. I knew what that meant as I shifted my gaze to the window. "I can't promise you that Miles will listen to me. They don't think I'm very... useful."

Caden was quiet for a moment. "What if the information came from Ivy?"

"They would listen. I can call her. Tonight."

"We also need to go to Tanner."

"Now?"

Caden clutched the steering wheel as he focused on the narrow street congested with cars and people. "Now. Call Tink. We'll pick him up."

I glanced down at myself as I pulled my cellphone out of my clutch. "Do we have, um, time for me to get changed?"

"Yeah, we've got time for that."

Calling Tink and getting off the phone quickly wasn't exactly an easy endeavor since he had a million and one questions, but I managed to get off and then I called Ivy.

She answered on the second ring. "Hey, Bri, what's up?"

"Um, a lot. Like a lot." I started quickly telling her about what had just gone down. "We're heading over to Hotel Good Fae now to talk to

Tanner and Faye."

"We're actually a couple of miles outside the city now," Ivy replied. "We'll be there shortly after you." There was a pause. "And I hope we find some time to talk later."

"About...?"

"You're going to play coy with me, Bri?" Ivy snorted. "You and I need to talk about how you've been working with the Prince."

"Uh." I looked over at Caden. He didn't seem to be paying attention. "Okay?"

"Yeah. Okay. See you in a bit."

I slipped my phone back into the clutch, unsure of what I was going to tell Ivy when I wasn't even sure I knew what I was doing—what we were doing.

"Is everything all right?"

I nodded. "Yeah, Ivy and Ren are almost back in the city. They'll be there. I guess your brother is with them."

"Perfect."

And after that, Caden didn't really speak and even though there was a ton of stuff I wanted to talk about, like *everything*, right now didn't seem like the... appropriate time. The curious thing about this trip was the fact that Caden didn't need to ask directions to my house.

"Do I want to know how you know where I live?" I asked as we pulled up to the curb outside my house.

He slid me a long look as he turned off the ignition.

"All right," I sighed, opening the door. "Probably don't want to know."

Stepping out of the SUV, I crossed the sidewalk and opened the gate. I took one step and Caden was suddenly in front of me. Cursing under my breath, I shook my head. "You're going to give me a heart attack if you keep doing that."

Caden didn't respond to that as he took my face in his hands, cupping my cheeks. He stepped into me as he tilted my head back. My gaze flew to his. "Is... is everything okay?"

Instead of answering, he lowered his mouth to mine, stopping a fraction of an inch from making contact. Was he going to kiss me? My breath caught. His forehead brushed mine and then his lips touched mine.

The kiss....

There was nothing sweet or soft about it, not like most first kisses were. Oh no, this was fierce and powerful, consuming in the intensity. My lips parted as the tip of his tongue touched mine, and the entire world seemed to slip away. When he finally lifted his mouth from mine, there was a swelling motion in my chest, like I had just taken my first real breath of air.

Caden had kissed me like it was our first and our last.

His fingertips slipped off my cheeks as he stepped back and to the side, and as my gaze focused, I saw that my front door was open. Tink stood there—full-sized Tink. It was always jarring to see him at his full height and wing-less, which was almost the size of Caden.

"Let's head inside." Caden touched the small of my back.

More than just a little out of it, I nodded and walked forward. The closer I got, I could see how wide Tink's blue eyes were. I expected him to say something funny. Call me a hussy or point out that I was just making out with Caden in the front yard, but he didn't say anything. He was staring at Caden like he'd never seen him before.

Tink stepped back into the foyer as we climbed the steps and he didn't speak until we were inside my house, the door closed behind us.

Tink looked like he was about to faint as he stared at Caden. "Should I... should I bow?"

I frowned at him.

Caden shook his head. "No."

I had no idea what any of that was about. "I'm just going to get changed real quick. Make yourself comfortable."

Caden nodded as I hurried to the stairs and when Tink started to follow, he stopped him. "Can we talk for a moment?"

Figuring it was about what happened, I raced up the steps, nearly tripping to my death over Dixon, who sprawled out on the top step. "God," I gasped. "Really?"

Dixon lifted his furry head and meowed loudly as he stretched out his legs lazily. Rolling my eyes, I stepped over the cat and hurried to my bedroom, prepared to strip and scrub my face so fast I'd break records, but as I soon as I stepped into my bedroom, I came to a complete stop. Raising my hand, I pressed my fingers to lips that felt swollen.

I... I was feeling some pretty silly stuff. Perhaps it was everything that had happened in the last week causing me to think and feel like I.... Goodness, I didn't even know.

But instead of obsessing over Aric, over what he'd taken part in, I was wondering if... you could fall in love with just one kiss?

Chapter 25

When I came back downstairs, dressed in the leggings and tunic I'd had on earlier and face scrubbed free of makeup, it was only Tink waiting for me, and it was jarring to see him full size. When Tink was what he liked to call "fun sized," he was just adorable, but fully grown? There was no way you could help acknowledging how attractive he was, and that just made me feel weird.

Frowning, I looked around the foyer. "Where's Caden?"

"He went ahead and is going to meet you in Tanner's office," he said in a voice so much deeper than what I was used to. "He left his car here for you to drive us."

"Oh." That was weird. "Did he fill you in on everything?"

"Most of it." Tink stepped toward me. "He… he kissed you."

Heat immediately smacked into my cheeks. "Yeah, he kind of did."

"He didn't kind of kiss you, Lite Bright. He looked like he was devouring your mouth."

It had kind of felt like that.

"Brighton, I…." Tink trailed off as he slowly shook his head.

A kernel of dread took root in my stomach. "What?"

"Nothing. We should go."

We really did need to get going, so when Tink handed me the keys that would allow me to drive Caden's SUV, I took them. That kernel of dread grew though when Tink was unnaturally quiet as he sat in the passenger seat. And Tink, even when he was full sized, was never quiet.

And he was almost never full-sized around me, not since, well, two years ago.

When we arrived at Hotel Good Fae, Tink headed off to the

cafeteria while I went to Tanner's office and waited for Caden. I had no idea how Tink stayed as fit as he did when I swore if he wasn't talking, he was eating something.

Must be brownie metabolism.

Taking a shallow breath, I roamed around Tanner's office, too antsy to sit down. Okay, I wasn't antsy. I was....

I was feeling a thousand different things. Disbelief. Anger. Shock, and then under that, under all of that, there was also anticipation.

Anticipation that had everything to do with Caden.

I rolled my eyes as I walked over to the window, ignoring the dull twinge in my side. There was a bubbling giddiness that made me feel *at least* a decade younger. Was that what love—

"Stop," I told myself and then I laughed, because telling myself to stop thinking what I'd already thought was kind of pointless.

I smoothed my hands over my hair, which felt weird against my neck. I was so used to wearing it up, but Caden had said....

He'd said he liked my hair down.

Actually, he'd used far more eloquent words than that. What had he said? My hair was like—

The door opened in that moment and I spun toward it.

Caden walked in, closing the door behind him, and as he looked over at me, seeming to know exactly where I stood, I got a little lost in... well, in staring at him.

Shamefully lost.

He'd changed, too. Wearing a white dress shirt tucked into a pair of tailored black slacks, he actually looked like a prince—a mouthwatering prince.

And he'd kissed me—really kissed me.

How crazy was that?

Totally insane.

Biting down on my lower lip, I tried to stop the grin from racing across my face so I didn't look crazy. I lost that battle as I started toward him, wanting to hug him—okay, I actually wanted to kiss him again. And I could do that, right? He'd kissed me and, well, he'd done more than that earlier, and—

"Do we have a moment?" he asked, and my smile slowly slipped from my face as I stopped. There was something... off about his tone. Empty. Cold? And his expression was utterly blank.

The sense of dread from the car ride rose as I swallowed. "Yeah, we have a couple of minutes."

His gaze flickered over my face before settling on the window. "I just wanted... to make sure we have an understanding between us."

"An understanding about what?" The dread gave way to a strange buzzing in my ears, adding a surreal element to all of this.

"About us."

I started to sit down, but found I couldn't move. "About us?" I repeated dumbly.

Still not looking at me, he nodded. "I know we have shared... intimacies, mostly under extreme circumstances, and we share this attraction."

Incapable of moving, all I could do was stand there as what felt like a fist reached into my chest and squeezed. That was how I knew what he was about to say. My heart already knew.

"I think you're incredibly brave, foolishly so at times," he continued, and a rush of prickly heat crept up the back of my neck. "You're intelligent and kind, and your beauty rivals that of the sun."

I sucked in a shaky breath. All of that sounded... sounded wonderful and beautiful and something I felt like I'd been waiting my whole life to hear, but...

I knew where this was going.

"Stop," I whispered, voice embarrassingly hoarse. "You don't have to do this."

"I do," he said, and I closed my eyes against the sudden, unwanted burn. "You are a treasure, Brighton."

"Okay," I laughed, the sound coarse to my own ears. "I'm a treasure?"

"You are." His voice softened.

I opened my eyes and I hated that. Hated how his expression wasn't void of emotion anymore. It was strained and tense and his gaze was conflicted.

Pressing my lips together, I dragged my hand through my hair as the wind seemed to whoosh out of my lungs.

"I don't want things to be awkward between us," he said, and another laugh crawled up my throat.

I turned back to him. "Why would it be awkward, *Caden?*"

He flinched at the sound of his name. "Because what we had, whatever that was, it wasn't real. It was an act that... that got out of hand."

There it was.

He wasn't beating around the bush anymore, but I didn't understand. I knew what he was saying, but it didn't make sense.

"You told me it was real." I managed to keep my voice steady. "You even called me out when I lied about how I felt. You said you wanted me. You just kissed me. You said you—"

"The physical part was real. How could it not be? You're beautiful and I'm—"

"And you're a man, and that's just how it goes? Really?" My eyes widened. "That's how you're going to play this? There was just a physical attraction and that's all?"

"I'm not playing anything. It's just the way it is." Caden turned from me, shoving a hand over his head, through his hair. "It's the way it needs to be. You're human and I'm—"

"I know what you are." My heart pounded in my chest as I folded my arms across my stomach. "I've always known what you are."

"Then you should know," he said.

"No, I don't. You just kissed—"

"I know I kissed you and that was—that was a stupid *mistake*."

"A mistake?" I whispered.

"Things have changed." His voice hardened now. "I don't want things to be uncomfortable between us. We need to work together. You need to put this behind us. I already have."

The hole in my chest cracked my heart as I stumbled back from him. I knew it shouldn't matter. I was just acknowledging that I had feelings for him—how deep those feelings ran, I didn't know—but there was a hole opening up in my chest.

There was no denying he meant what he said. I heard it in his voice. I saw it in his face, and I had no idea how I'd misread things with him so badly. How I could've been so damn foolish to think there was more to what was between us.

Humiliation festered to life, settling into my bones and spreading like a fever, flushing my skin.

Caden—no, he wasn't Caden to me anymore. He was just the Prince, and he must've sensed the sharp, bitter swirl of emotions churning through me, because he stepped toward me.

"Brighton—"

"I get it." I cut him off as I stepped to the side. "Message received."

"I'm—"

"Don't apologize. God, please don't apologize. That's...." When his face began to blur I knew I needed to get out of this room. I would not lose it in front of him. I would not cry over what could have been when there was apparently nothing in the first place. "You said... you said you wouldn't hurt me. You lied."

He drew back as if I'd hit him.

"I need to go," I said.

And I did.

Ivy and Ren would've been here by now, waiting for us in the main common area, and I just... I just needed to get the hell out of this room.

Giving him a wide berth, I skirted around the chairs and made a beeline for the door. I made it and I made it out into the empty hallway knowing that the Prince could've stopped me at any moment.

But he hadn't.

He'd chosen not to.

Acknowledging that hollowed out my chest, and I walked to the common area in a daze, focused only on breathing around the burn in my throat.

Hands shaking, I kept them fisted tight as I picked up my pace, reaching the main hall. There were fae everywhere. They spilled out from the common area, their eyes wide and the hum of excitement charged the room.

I had no idea what was going on as I scanned the unfamiliar faces. There was a shock of red hair toward the back. *Ivy*. She and Ren were here, which meant that was probably where Tink was. Concentrating only on getting to them, I didn't notice the first fae to drop to their knee before me.

But then they went down in a wave, one after the other, dropping to their knees and bowing deeply, placing their right hands on the floor. All of them went down until I could see Ivy standing near the entrance to the common room and beside her was Ren. Both looked surprised as I felt.

Neither of them looked as shocked as Prince Fabian, though, which was saying something because both Ren and Ivy looked about as confused as I felt.

Prince Fabian's long blond hair was pulled back, revealing just how pale his face was as his lips moved wordlessly.

Then he dropped to his right knee and placed his right hand onto the floor.

"What the hell?" I whispered, turning around slowly, knowing they weren't bowing for me, because duh.

Things are different now.

I saw him in the hall I'd just hurried out of, the edges of his blond hair brushing those wide shoulders and those odd amber eyes were not on the fae who were bowing to him but on me.

"Oh my God," I whispered as Tink's words from the night the Prince was wounded came back to me in a rush. *If he dies, then Fabian becomes King and he... he can't be King.*

Did that mean...?

He closed his eyes and a reddish-yellow glow appeared, just like it had before, as if there was a halo of light behind him. There was no flaming sword this time when the glow receded.

Instead there was a burnt gold crown atop his head.

Caden was no longer the Prince.

He was the King.

* * * *

Also from 1001 Dark Nights and Jennifer L. Armentrout, discover The King and Dream of You.

Sign up for the 1001 Dark Nights Newsletter
and be entered to win a Tiffany Key necklace.

There's a contest every month!

Go to www.1001DarkNights.com to subscribe.

As a bonus, all subscribers will receive a free copy of
Discovery Bundle Three
Featuring stories by
Sidney Bristol, Darcy Burke, T. Gephart
Stacey Kennedy, Adriana Locke
JB Salsbury, and Erika Wilde

Discover 1001 Dark Nights Collection Five

Go to www.1001DarkNights.com for more information

BLAZE ERUPTING by Rebecca Zanetti
Scorpius Syndrome/A Brigade Novella

ROUGH RIDE by Kristen Ashley
A Chaos Novella

HAWKYN by Larissa Ione
A Demonica Underworld Novella

RIDE DIRTY by Laura Kaye
A Raven Riders Novella

ROME'S CHANCE by Joanna Wylde
A Reapers MC Novella

THE MARRIAGE ARRANGEMENT by Jennifer Probst
A Marriage to a Billionaire Novella

SURRENDER by Elisabeth Naughton
A House of Sin Novella

INKED NIGHT by Carrie Ann Ryan
A Montgomery Ink Novella

ENVY by Rachel Van Dyken
An Eagle Elite Novella

PROTECTED by Lexi Blake
A Masters and Mercenaries Novella

THE PRINCE by Jennifer L. Armentrout
A Wicked Novella

PLEASE ME by J. Kenner
A Stark Ever After Novella

Discover 1001 Dark Nights Collection One

Go to www.1001DarkNights.com for more information

FOREVER WICKED by Shayla Black
CRIMSON TWILIGHT by Heather Graham
CAPTURED IN SURRENDER by Liliana Hart
SILENT BITE: A SCANGUARDS WEDDING by Tina Folsom
DUNGEON GAMES by Lexi Blake
AZAGOTH by Larissa Ione
NEED YOU NOW by Lisa Renee Jones
SHOW ME, BABY by Cherise Sinclair
ROPED IN by Lorelei James
TEMPTED BY MIDNIGHT by Lara Adrian
THE FLAME by Christopher Rice
CARESS OF DARKNESS by Julie Kenner

Also from 1001 Dark Nights

TAME ME by J. Kenner

Discover 1001 Dark Nights Collection Two

Go to www.1001DarkNights.com for more information

WICKED WOLF by Carrie Ann Ryan
WHEN IRISH EYES ARE HAUNTING by Heather Graham
EASY WITH YOU by Kristen Proby
MASTER OF FREEDOM by Cherise Sinclair
CARESS OF PLEASURE by Julie Kenner
ADORED by Lexi Blake
HADES by Larissa Ione
RAVAGED by Elisabeth Naughton
DREAM OF YOU by Jennifer L. Armentrout
STRIPPED DOWN by Lorelei James
RAGE/KILLIAN by Alexandra Ivy/Laura Wright
DRAGON KING by Donna Grant
PURE WICKED by Shayla Black
HARD AS STEEL by Laura Kaye
STROKE OF MIDNIGHT by Lara Adrian
ALL HALLOWS EVE by Heather Graham
KISS THE FLAME by Christopher Rice
DARING HER LOVE by Melissa Foster
TEASED by Rebecca Zanetti
THE PROMISE OF SURRENDER by Liliana Hart

Also from 1001 Dark Nights

THE SURRENDER GATE By Christopher Rice
SERVICING THE TARGET By Cherise Sinclair

Discover 1001 Dark Nights Collection Three

Go to www.1001DarkNights.com for more information

HIDDEN INK by Carrie Ann Ryan
BLOOD ON THE BAYOU by Heather Graham
SEARCHING FOR MINE by Jennifer Probst
DANCE OF DESIRE by Christopher Rice
ROUGH RHYTHM by Tessa Bailey
DEVOTED by Lexi Blake
Z by Larissa Ione
FALLING UNDER YOU by Laurelin Paige
EASY FOR KEEPS by Kristen Proby
UNCHAINED by Elisabeth Naughton
HARD TO SERVE by Laura Kaye
DRAGON FEVER by Donna Grant
KAYDEN/SIMON by Alexandra Ivy/Laura Wright
STRUNG UP by Lorelei James
MIDNIGHT UNTAMED by Lara Adrian
TRICKED by Rebecca Zanetti
DIRTY WICKED by Shayla Black
THE ONLY ONE by Lauren Blakely
SWEET SURRENDER by Liliana Hart

Discover 1001 Dark Nights Collection Four

Go to www.1001DarkNights.com for more information

ROCK CHICK REAWAKENING by Kristen Ashley
ADORING INK by Carrie Ann Ryan
SWEET RIVALRY by K. Bromberg
SHADE'S LADY by Joanna Wylde
RAZR by Larissa Ione
ARRANGED by Lexi Blake
TANGLED by Rebecca Zanetti
HOLD ME by J. Kenner
SOMEHOW, SOME WAY by Jennifer Probst
TOO CLOSE TO CALL by Tessa Bailey
HUNTED by Elisabeth Naughton
EYES ON YOU by Laura Kaye
BLADE by Alexandra Ivy/Laura Wright
DRAGON BURN by Donna Grant
TRIPPED OUT by Lorelei James
STUD FINDER by Lauren Blakely
MIDNIGHT UNLEASHED by Lara Adrian
HALLOW BE THE HAUNT by Heather Graham
DIRTY FILTHY FIX by Laurelin Paige
THE BED MATE by Kendall Ryan
PRINCE ROMAN by CD Reiss
NO RESERVATIONS by Kristen Proby
DAWN OF SURRENDER by Liliana Hart

Also from 1001 Dark Nights

Tempt Me by J. Kenner

About Jennifer L. Armentrout

1 New York Times and International Bestselling author Jennifer lives in Martinsburg, West Virginia. All the rumors you've heard about her state aren't true. When she's not hard at work writing. she spends her time reading, watching really bad zombie movies, pretending to write, and hanging out with her husband and her Jack Russell Loki.

Her dreams of becoming an author started in algebra class, where she spent most of her time writing short stories…which explains her dismal grades in math. Jennifer writes young adult paranormal, science fiction, fantasy, and contemporary romance. She is published with Tor Teen, Entangled Teen and Brazen, Disney/Hyperion and Harlequin Teen. Her book *Wicked* has been optioned by Passionflix and slated to begin filming in late 2018. Her young adult romantic suspense novel *DON'T LOOK BACK* was a 2014 nominated Best in Young Adult Fiction by YALSA and her novel *THE PROBLEM WITH FOREVER* is a 2017 RITA Award winning novel.

She also writes Adult and New Adult contemporary and paranormal romance under the name J. Lynn. She is published by Entangled Brazen and HarperCollins.

Discover More Jennifer L. Armentrout

The King: A Wicked Novella
By Jennifer L. Armentrout
Coming July 23, 2019

From #1 New York Times and USA Today bestselling author Jennifer L. Armentrout comes the next installment in her Wicked series.

As Caden and Brighton's attraction grows despite the odds stacked against a happily ever after, they must work together to stop an Ancient fae from releasing the Queen, who wants nothing more than to see Caden become the evil Prince once feared by fae and mortals alike.

* * * *

Dream of You: A Wait For You Novella
By Jennifer L. Armentrout
Now available.

Abby Erickson isn't looking for a one-night stand, a relationship, or anything that involves any one-on-one time, but when she witnesses a shocking crime, she's thrust into the hands of the sexiest man she's ever seen - Colton Anders. His job is to protect her, but with every look, every touch, and every simmering kiss, she's in danger of not only losing her life but her heart also.

On behalf of 1001 Dark Nights,

Liz Berry and M.J. Rose would like to thank ~

Steve Berry
Doug Scofield
Kim Guidroz
Jillian Stein
InkSlinger PR
Dan Slater
Asha Hossain
Chris Graham
Fedora Chen
Kasi Alexander
Jessica Johns
Dylan Stockton
Richard Blake
and Simon Lipskar